Shuffle the Shoemaker

Enid Blyton
Pictures by Thomas Taylor

SIENA

Shuffle the Shoemaker was first published as
Rubbalong Tales by Macmillan & Co in 1950
First Published by Bloomsbury Publishing Plc in 1997
38 Soho Square, London W1V 5DF

This edition is for Siena,
13 Whiteladies Road, Clifton, Bristol BS8 1PB

Gnid Blyton

The moral right of the author and illustrator has been asserted
A CIP catalogue record of this book is available from the
British Library

ISBN 0 75252 794 0

Printed in Great Britain by Clays Ltd, St Ives plc

10 9 8 7 6 5 4 3 2 1

Cover design by Mandy Sherliker

Contents

Chapter 1

Shuffle Takes a Chance

'Well, here we are, Ma!' said little Shuffle, and he put his mother's heavy trunk down on the floor of the tiny cottage they had just come to live in. 'Now you just settle in, and I'll look round for a job of work!'

'I don't know how we're going to live, the two of us, in a place we don't know,' said his mother.

'Oh, we're sure to get along,' said Shuffle. 'Don't you worry about that, Ma! I'll just go round and see if I can get any boots and shoes to mend. See you soon.'

Off he went, whistling. He went to the market-place and kept his eyes open, and listened to all that was going on with his big pointed ears.

Soon he saw a grand carriage draw up, and out got an important-looking person, followed by his wife.

'That's Mr Tuck-In and his wife,' whispered somebody near Shuffle. 'Richest man in Tiptop Village!'

'He may be rich – but look at his shoes!' said Shuffle. 'Down at heel and dirty – and his wife's shoes are the same. What a shocking thing!'

He stepped boldly up to Mr Tuck-In . 'Sir!

I see you need your shoes mending,' said little Shuffle. 'May I have the honour of doing them for you?'

'Certainly not,' said Mr Tuck-In, pushing him away. 'Don't be impertinent.'

'I'm not, sir. I'm just somebody who's looking for a chance,' said Shuffle.

'I don't give people chances,' said Mr Tuck-In.

He disappeared into a shop. Shuffle spoke to the person next to him. 'Do you know much about him or his wife?'

'No,' said the little man nearby. 'Except that his wife hates cats! *That* bit of news won't help you!'

'It might! Yes, it might!' said Shuffle, and he went off home to his mother, thinking so hard that he fell over one of her cats on the doorstep.

'Mee-OW,' said the cat crossly.

'Ma! May I borrow your three cats for tonight?' called Shuffle. His mother looked amazed.

'Borrow Tib, Tab and Tubby? You must be mad!' she said. 'Whatever for?'

'You'll see tomorrow,' said Shuffle with a grin. And that night he borrowed the three cats and made them come with him to Mr Tuck-In's big garden.

'Now sing,' he ordered the cats. 'SING! Go on.'

It wasn't often that anyone wanted Tib, Tab and Tubby to sing. Why, this was wonderful. The three cats sat down, threw back their furry heads, opened their mouths and caterwauled.

'Mee-ow, ee-ow-eeow! Me-OOOOO! Hark at mee-ow-ow! Do-ray-meeeeeeee-OW!'

Well, you never heard such a noise in your life! Up went the Tuck-Ins' window, and Mrs Tuck-In looked out angrily.

'Shoo! Shush! Go away, you miseries!'

'Sing louder!' whispered Shuffle, and Tib, Tab and Tubby obliged at once.

'You just wait!' shouted Mrs Tuck-In, and she disappeared into her bedroom. She came to the window again with an old shoe. Wheeee! It flew through the air, and the cats looked startled.

'Take no notice!' said Shuffle. 'Sing again.'

So they sang, and out of that window came shouts and yells and dozens of boots and shoes and even Mr Tuck-In's best hat that Mrs Tuck-In had picked up by mistake!

Plunk! Thud! Crash! Bang! Out they all came one after the other and the cats wanted to run away. Shuffle let them go at last. He felt certain there couldn't be any more boots and shoes left in the bedroom!

He gathered them all up. He ran home. He lit his little candle, and sat down at his last. He worked all night long – mending this heel, and that sole, hammering and whistling all the night till his mother nearly went mad.

'A new lace here – and two new buttons there – and a new pompon for that dance-shoe, and we're done!' said little Shuffle. He finished his work and set out all the shoes and boots in a row. He polished every one till they all shone brilliantly. He even brushed Mr Tuck-In's hat and put a new ribbon round it.

Next morning he put everything into a big basket and went round to Mr Tuck-In's. There was a tremendous row going on there.

'Do you mean to say you've thrown *all* my boots and shoes into the garden at those cats? And do you mean to tell me that some tramp has taken the lot? What, you threw my best hat, too? Are you MAD?'

Shuffle walked in at this very minute, beaming.

'Good morning, Mr Tuck-In, sir. I found all your boots and shoes and your hat, too, in your garden. Here they are!'

He set them out in a row. Mr and Mrs Tuck-In gazed at them in silence. Mr Tuck-In's eyes almost popped out of his head.

'Are those really mine?' he said. 'How beautiful they look! What a clever little cobbler you must be!'

'I only wanted a chance,' said Shuffle modestly. 'There's nothing to pay, sir, if you don't want to pay. You didn't give me the job. I took it!'

'Then take this, too!' said Mr Tuck-In, and he handed Shuffle five shining pieces of gold. 'I like a fellow who takes a chance when he sees one, and makes something good out of it. Thank you very much. I'll tell all my friends about you!'

'Very good of you, Mr Tuck-In, sir,' said Shuffle, and bowed himself out.

Mrs Tuck-In looked at Mr Tuck-In. 'Did you know that Ma Shuffle has three cats?' she said suddenly. 'I can't help thinking they had something to do with all this.'

'You've got cats on the brain,' said Mr Tuck-In, pulling on a shining boot. 'Good little Shuffle. He certainly deserved a chance.'

Well, he did, didn't he?

Chapter 2

Grabbit Meets his Match

Little Shuffle was really getting along very well. He had set up a very fine business as a cobbler in Tiptop Village. Mr Tuck-In had kept his word and had told all his friends about him.

'Look here, Ma,' said Shuffle one morning, and he showed her a wooden box. He unlocked it – and inside were a great many gold and silver coins. 'See how much I've saved already!'

'Not bad,' said Ma Shuffle. 'Count it up and we'll see how much we have. Perhaps we shall be able to have a new roof put on our cottage soon. The rain does come in so badly!'

They were in the middle of counting the

money when Mrs Well-I-Never came into the room with a pair of old shoes for mending. Her eyes nearly fell out of her head when she saw so much money.

'Well, I never!' she said. 'No, don't hide it away from me. I won't tell a soul.'

'Don't you go and tell that rogue of a brother of yours,' said Mrs Shuffle at once. 'He sniffs money just like a dog sniffing out a rat.'

'Well, I never! Fancy thinking I'd tell my brother Grabbit!' said the old woman, and she flounced out of the cottage in a huff.

Now the very next day there came a message from Grabbit: 'Please call for my shoes. They need soling.'

'Well, you just *won't* call for them, Shuffle,' said his mother firmly. 'He'd take every penny out of your pockets. I guess Mrs Well-I-Never has told him you've got money saved up.'

'Now, Ma – you don't suppose I'm going to fill my pockets with money when I fetch Grabbit's shoes, do you?' said Shuffle getting up. 'I'll go and deliver all the shoes I've mended, and then I'll call at Grabbit's and get his – and I don't mind telling you he'll have to pay me a fine big price for doing them!'

'You be careful,' said Ma Shuffle. 'You're not as clever as you think you are!'

'Oh, but I am!' said little Shuffle, and off he went.

He delivered all the boots and shoes, and was paid for them. Oh dear – now he had money in his pockets after all! He wouldn't tell Grabbit, of course – he wouldn't even let his money jingle or clink.

It was a long way to Grabbit's, and by the time he got there it was dark. Shuffle banged at the door. Blim-blam. It opened, and there was Grabbit.

He was an ugly-looking fellow, with eyes hidden under shaggy eyebrows, and long, swinging arms that looked ready to grab at anything.

He grabbed at Shuffle and dragged him into his cottage. In a trice he had all Shuffle's money out of his pockets and into his own.

'Stop that!' cried Shuffle, sounding much braver than he felt. 'Give me back my money.'

'You're going to give me some *more*, little

Shuffle; yes, some *more*,' said Grabbit, in his wheezy voice. 'My sister told me how rich you are. You take me to your cottage and let me have that box. Or do you want to be turned into a blackcurrant lozenge and given to someone with a cough?'

Shuffle was very frightened. 'Let me go,' he said. 'You come to my cottage some other time and I'll give you some of my money. But let me go now!'

'I don't know where you live,' said Grabbit. 'Come on – take me!'

Shuffle got up. A sudden little gleam came into his eye. Grabbit took firm hold of his arm.

'This way,' said Shuffle, going down the path. 'Now *that* way – and then up the hill. Come along.'

Grabbit went with him, thinking of all the money he would get from Shuffle's wooden box. Oho!

They came to the top of the hill. A strange little round house stood there all by itself, half lost in the darkness.

'There you are!' said Shuffle. 'Go along in. Knock at the door first.'

Grabbit marched up to the door. How clever he was! He could get money from any-one! He knocked at the door. BLIM-BLAM-CRASH.

He threw open the door with a bang. He strode into the room beyond, and there he saw an old dame sitting, stirring a big black pot. He thought it must be Shuffle's mother.

'Where's that money?' he shouted.

'How *dare* you come marching into my house like this!' cried the old woman. 'I'll teach you to come here demanding money!'

And she caught up a stick and gave

Grabbit such a prod with it that he fell over backwards into the big pot. Every time he tried to get out she pushed him back.

'I'll teach you what happens to people who come and shout at Old Dame Dandy!' she cried. Grabbit looked at her in great alarm.

'Aren't you – aren't you Ma Shuffle, then?' he asked.

'No! I tell you I'm Dame Dandy, who even the greatest enchanters are afraid of,' said the old woman. 'Silly of you to come to my cottage, wasn't it?'

Well, it certainly was. Shuffle laughed till he cried when he peeped in at the window. In he went, and got back his money when he had told Dame Dandy his tale.

'Grabbit's fallen into a Blue Spell I'm making,' said Dame Dandy. 'He will be a sight!'

He was. You should just see him walking round with a blue face and blue hands and blue hair.

He feels blue, too!

Chapter 3

Shuffle Gets a Shock . . .

'It seems to me, Ma, that Button the Brownie is taking some of my customers,' said little Shuffle one day, when nobody had brought any shoes or boots to be mended.

'Maybe he is,' said Ma Shuffle. 'He doesn't charge as much as you do.'

'Well, but my work is better,' said Shuffle. 'You know it is.'

'You go and talk to him,' said Ma Shuffle. 'There's plenty of work for you both. But be polite now, Shuffle, and don't lose your temper. A smile goes further than a frown!'

Shuffle smiled and his frown disappeared. But it soon came back again when he arrived at Button's house. Button was just taking a pair of shoes from Mr Tuck-In.

'You're a mean little cheat,' said Shuffle fiercely. 'Taking my customers like this!'

'I've got to live, haven't I?' said Button cheekily. 'And don't you call me names, Shuffle. I know plenty of magic, and I'll soon wish you at the top of a high tree somewhere if you're rude.'

'*You* know magic?' cried Shuffle disbelievingly. 'Why, you don't even know how to put a shoe-heel on properly. I know a hundred times more magic than you do.'

'OOOOOH – fibber!' said Button. 'I'll turn you into a pack of cards and shuffle you – ho, ho, Shuffle getting shuffled – that's a good joke, that is!'

'And I'll turn you into a button, and button you up!' shouted Shuffle. 'That's a better joke – go on, turn into a button!'

And Shuffle made the magic sign as he spoke. Hey presto, Button disappeared – and there, on his stool, lay a bright little red button, winking in the sun.

Shuffle chuckled. He picked it up and put it in his pocket. 'Got you!' he said, and was just about to go out when he heard Button's mother coming.

'Hello, Shuffle,' said Mrs Button. 'How

nice to see you! Button was saying yesterday that we really must ask you to tea. He's very fond of you, you know.'

'Is he?' said Shuffle, feeling awkward. 'Well – I must be going.'

'No – stay and have a bit of new-made cake with me and Button,' begged little Mrs Button. 'Button, BUTTON! Where are you? Here's your old friend Shuffle.'

Shuffle couldn't bear this. He felt that he really must rush out into a corner and change Button back again to his own shape at once. He was dreadfully sorry he had been so silly.

He rushed out, down the path, and along the road. He came to some trees and stopped under them. He felt in his pocket for the little red button.

But it wasn't there! There was a hole in his pocket. The button must have dropped out.

'Blow! Bother! Where's he gone?' groaned Shuffle, and ran back up the road. He met Mrs Well-I-Never.

'Lost something?' she asked. 'Oh – a red button. Well, I never! I saw Mr Tuck-In pick it up a moment ago!'

'Thank you, thank you!' cried little Shuffle, and rushed after Mr Tuck-In. He found him in Mrs Doodle's house, visiting her husband.

'Mr Tuck-In, sir! Did you find a little red button in the road just now?' asked Shuffle anxiously.

'Yes, I did,' said Mr Tuck-In, surprised. 'Was it yours? Oh, dear – I gave it to the little girl next door.'

'Oh, my!' wailed Shuffle, and rushed out of the house at once. He went next door and knocked loudly. A woman answered the door.

'Where's your little girl?' panted Shuffle. 'She's got a button of mine. I simply must get it. It's most important.'

'A button? *I* didn't know she'd got some-body's button,' said the woman. 'She's gone down to the shops, I think.'

Shuffle fled down to the shops. He found the little girl. 'Where's that button?' he asked her. 'The red one Mr Tuck-In gave you. I'll buy you an ice-cream if you'll give it to me.'

'Oh – I gave it to Tiggy the goblin boy,' said the little girl. 'He liked it because it was red. He gave me this shell for it. Would you like that?'

'No, no,' cried poor Shuffle and tore down the street to look for Tiggy. He found him at last, sitting on the kerb, playing with coloured marbles, buttons and stones.

But the little red button wasn't there. Shuffle nearly wept. 'What have you done with that little red button?' he asked Tiggy. '*Don't* say you've swallowed it! I couldn't bear it!'

'No. An old woman came by, and she saw the button, and she said it would match some others she'd got on a coat,' said Tiggy, surprised. 'She gave me a penny for it, look!'

'Who was the old woman?' asked Shuffle. But Tiggy didn't know. So, feeling very sad, very worried, and very much ashamed of himself, Shuffle went home. He walked gloomily into his kitchen and sat down on his stool.

'What's the matter?' said Ma Shuffle, who was sitting behind a pile of mending.

Shuffle burst into tears. 'I daren't tell you what I've done, Ma. I'm bad. I'm wicked!'

'Don't be silly,' said Ma Shuffle. 'Take off that coat of yours, and let me mend the hole in it. Put this one on instead.'

She held out his other coat. Shuffle gave a doleful sniff and held out his hand for it. Then he stared and stared! He gave a yell.

'Ma! Ma! Where did you get this red button – the one you've sewn on my coat?'

'From Tiggy,' said his mother, astonished.

'MA! Do you know what you've done? You've sewn Button the Brownie on to my coat!' shouted Shuffle. 'Oh, Button, dear Button – I'll change you back again now. Do, do forgive me! Oh, to think you've been sewn on my coat! Oh Ma, Ma, look what you've done!'

Well, in a trice the red button was changed back into Button the Brownie. And was he angry? Was he furious? No – he laughed and laughed. And after a bit Shuffle laughed, too, and so did Ma.

Ma Shuffle wiped her eyes. 'It's all come right *this* time! she said. 'But any more nonsense from you two, and *I'll* do a bit of magic – I'll turn you into a couple of mats and put you on the line and beat you!'

And she would, too!

Chapter 4

Mr Stamp-About

Once Mr Stamp-About came to stay with his sister, Dame Scary, in Tiptop Village.

He stamped into her little house and it shook from roof to floor. He banged his bag down in the hall and yelled for his sister.

'Hey, Scary! I've come to stay!'

His sister wasn't pleased. She was a quiet, timid little woman, and she didn't like selfish people with loud voices, bad tempers and stamping feet. She came running out of the kitchen.

'Oh, Stamp-About! Why didn't you tell me you were coming?'

Stamp-About grinned. 'Still the same scary little mouse, aren't you?' he said. 'It'll do you good to have me stamping about the place.'

But it didn't do Dame Scary any good. Bang! That was Stamp-About slamming a door. Crash! That was a boot being flung across the floor. Eeeee-ow! That was Dame Scary's cat trying to get out of the way.

Nobody liked Stamp-About. He was so full of himself, so sure he was right. He shouted everyone down, he wanted the best of everything. Poor little Dame Scary got to look so like a timid mouse that when Ma Shuffle met her one day she quite expected to see her growing whiskers and a tail.

'It's that brother of mine,' whispered Dame Scary. 'He says he livens up the house – but all he does is to make me feel half dead. If only he'd go away, and never come back.'

'People like Stamp-About never do go away,' said Ma Shuffle. 'Nobody can get rid of them. All I hope is that he won't come and see *us*. You know what little Shuffle is – he'll be cheeky to Stamp-About if he comes stamping into *my* little house. He'll tell him he doesn't serve elephants.'

'Oh, dear,' cried Dame Scary, 'I'm afraid he *is* coming to see Shuffle. You see, he stamps about so much that he wears his boots out remarkably quickly.'

'I see,' said Ma Shuffle. 'You mean he wants Shuffle to mend them? Well, he won't."

Stamp-About strode into Shuffle's little cottage that very day, and fell over the three cats on the doorstep.

He roared. 'Cats! Cats everywhere! Shuffle, where are you? I've brought all my boots for you to mend.'

'Sorry. Too busy,' said little Shuffle, not even looking up from his work.

'Nobody's too busy to work for me,' said Stamp-About in a rage, and he began to stamp up and down the little room so fiercely that the kettle fell off the hob and the kitchen clock jigged up and down on the dresser.

'Put the kettle back, please,' said Shuffle, feeling a bit like a kettle himself, ready to boil over.

Stamp-About looked at little Shuffle in angry surprise.

'Look at me all you like,' said Shuffle. 'You won't see a better cobbler than I am! And I can make the finest shoes in the country.

Why – I'm even making a pair to present to the king!'

Stamp-About was surprised. He looked round the kitchen and saw a magnificent pair of shoes, almost finished. They were red, made of the finest leather, and had silver laces.

'*I'll* buy those shoes,' said Stamp-About at once. 'Now look here, no more nonsense, Shuffle. You mend all my boots for me and

I'll pay you double – and I'll buy those new shoes for ten gold pieces. I'll come for them tomorrow.'

Shuffle looked up. 'Very well – I'll mend the boots for double the price, because I'm charging you for your rudeness, too. But as for those red shoes, you can't have them.'

'We'll see about that,' said Stamp-About, beginning to lose his temper. He went out, fell over the cats again, and stamped down the street, shouting at every child he met.

'What a toad!' said Ma Shuffle, appearing from the scullery. 'Don't you mend those boots of his, Shuffle.'

'Ma – I want a Walk-Away Spell,' said Shuffle. 'Can you make me one?'

'Now, what in the world do you want that for?' said his mother, but Shuffle wouldn't tell her. He mended all Stamp-About's boots and took them along to him that night.

But, of course, Stamp-About wouldn't pay him. He took the boots and slammed the door in Shuffle's face. Shuffle grinned slyly.

'Hey, Stamp-About – you won't get the king's shoes now – serves you right!'

Stamp-About's big face appeared at the window. 'Oho! You wait and see!'

That night Shuffle took a little green spell from his mother and shook it, all powdery and bright, into the fine red shoes. Then he hid in the boot cupboard and waited.

Sh! What was that? Someone opening the window! Someone slinking in. Someone groping for the king's shoes. Someone pulling them on!

And then a loud voice rang out. 'Ho, there, Shuffle! I've got the shoes!'

And out stamped Stamp-About, roaring with laughter. Shuffle laughed, too. He called his mother and they ran out into the moonlight. Faces appeared at windows as Stamp-About strode down the street, singing loudly.

Shuffle did a little dance in the middle of the street. 'He's got a Walk-Away Spell in his shoes! He can't stop walking!' he shouted. 'We're rid of him forever!'

So they were. Stamp-About had to walk till the shoes fell to pieces – and by that time he was in the Land of Far-Far-Away, and couldn't come back.

Well, well, little Shuffle, there's no getting the better of *you*!

Chapter 5

Mischief in the Kitchen

Shuffle was going through Ding-Dong Wood, a pair of boots hung round his neck to take home to mend.

He suddenly heard a loud howl. 'Don't! Don't! Oh, my lovely hat!'

He ran down the path and peeped round a tree. He saw Sniff, a small goblin, grinning at two brownie children. They were howling dismally.

Shuffle saw why. Sniff had waylaid the children, and played a trick on them. He had thrown both their hats high up in the tree. Nasty little Sniff! He's always doing things like that.

Shuffle grinned. He strolled round the tree. 'Hello! Nice game this you're playing

Sniff. Can I play it, too?'

And before Sniff could say a word he snatched off his feathered goblin-hat and flung it up to the topmost branch of the nearby tree. Then he pulled off Sniff's coat and threw that up, too, then his belt and his shoes. There they all hung, jigging in the wind that shook the tree.

'Nice game! Really exciting!' said Shuffle. 'So glad you let me play it, too. So long, Sniff. Come on, children – I'll take you home.'

Now, a few days after that, very peculiar things began to happen to Shuffle and his old mother. The kitchen clock jumped down to the floor and every time it was put back it jumped down again.

Then the poker walked out into the middle of the room and back again. Once it even poked at one of the cats.

When Ma Shuffle was baking cakes, the oven door kept opening and shutting, and all her cakes were spoilt. The kettle behaved strangely, too – it would keep tipping itself up and pouring water on to the three cats on the hearth rug.

'Ma! I don't like this,' said Shuffle in alarm. 'Has one of your spells got loose?'

'Maybe it's a Fidgety Spell got loose,' said
Ma Shuffle puzzled. But no – all her spells
were safe.

Then the dustbin out in the yard went
mad. It kept leaving its place and coming to
the window and looking in. It even said
things.

'I'm waiting for you, Shuffle,' it said in a
tinny voice, and jiggled its lid. 'I take in rubbish – and that's why I'm waiting for you.'

'How awfully *rude*,' said Shuffle, and put the dustbin back into its place. 'Be civil,' he said to it. 'And stay put.'

But it didn't stay put and one night it kept Shuffle and his mother awake for hours because it jiggled its lid without stopping.

Then the three cats went mad, too. Tib suddenly leapt into the air as if somebody had run a pin into her. Tab suddenly jumped out of the window and ran for miles. Tubby woke up with a yowl and tore round the room without stopping.

'What's happening?' said little Shuffle, more alarmed than ever. 'Ma, I don't like it. There *is* a spell running about loose here. We'd better move.'

'Move! When we've only just come!' said Ma Shuffle. 'No, my boy. It's the spell that will have to move. It's . . . ooooooooooooh!'

Ma! What's the matter?' cried Shuffle as his mother shot up from her chair.

'Something bit me,' said Ma Shuffle, and showed him her hand. 'Just there. That's no spell, Shuffle. Spells don't have teeth.'

'No. It's some invisible imp or goblin,' said Shuffle fiercely, and he stared all round. 'Where are you, you misery? Show yourself!'

He heard a squeal of laughter from the dresser, and the dishes on the top shelf began to roll to and fro.

Shuffle lunged out, hoping to catch who-ever was sitting on the shelf, but he couldn't feel anyone. Another squeal came from behind him, and when he turned round quickly he saw all the boots and shoes he was mending flying up into the air, one after another.

'Ma! What are we going to do?' cried little Shuffle. 'Ma – your hair's coming down – and your apron-string's undone. Ma, your – '

'Hold your tongue,' said Ma Shuffle. 'I want to think. Bless us, there goes that dustbin again! If I see it peeping into the window any more I'll go mad.'

'Ma – whoever's playing these tricks on us is out in the yard now, moving the dustbin,' said Shuffle in a whisper. 'Quick, Ma – make a plan.'

'Yes – yes – I've got a plan,' said Ma Shuffle, tying her apron-string. 'Get me the pepper-pot, Shuffle – the big one. And as soon as anything peculiar happens in the kitchen, shut all the windows and doors at once, so that we'll know the imp is here. Then watch your chance!'

Shuffle grinned. He fetched the big pepper-pot. His mother hid it under her apron. They waited. Then the clock jumped down to the floor, so they knew that the joker was in the kitchen again.

Shuffle slammed the door shut. He shut the windows. Ma Shuffle whipped the pepper-pot out from under her apron and began to shake it hard into every corner. She and Shuffle held their noses – and they listened.

'A-whooosh-oo!' What a sneeze! It came from under the table. Shuffle flung himself there – no, he didn't catch anyone.

'AWHHOOOOOOOSH-oooo!' Aha – that was over in the corner. Ma Shuffle and Shuffle both grabbed at the air there.

And they caught someone – someone

small and wriggly, who became visible as soon as Ma Shuffle sprinkled him with hot water.

'It's Sniff!' cried Shuffle. 'Sniff the Goblin! I might have guessed it. Ma, he played these tricks just because I punished him for teasing children. The nasty, spiteful little creature! I really don't know what we're going to do with him.'

But Ma Shuffle knew all right. She gave Sniff one of her very, very best scoldings.

You'll hardly believe it, but the dustbin was so interested that it almost broke the window, trying to watch. I'm not surprised. It's always good to know that somebody is getting what he deserves.

Chapter 6

Walls Have Ears,
and Shoes Have Tongues

'Now look here, Ma,' said little Shuffle, 'I'm not going to mend Mrs Shifty's shoes any more – no, not even if she *did* go to school with you years and years ago!'

'Hasn't she paid her bill yet?' said Ma Shuffle, busily rubbing her kitchen stove till it shone like silver. 'Well, well – Shifty by name, and shifty by nature, I suppose. Give her another chance, Shuffle.'

'No, Ma,' said Shuffle. 'I've mended seven pairs of shoes, and not one pair has she paid me for.'

'Give me that pair she left with you yesterday,' said Ma Shuffle suddenly. She stopped cleaning her stove and held out her hand for them. 'Are these hers? Now, listen, Shuffle –

I want five minutes alone with these shoes –
and then I want you to mend them. And I
promise you she'll pay for them – and all the
rest as well!'

'What are you up to now, Ma?' said little
Shuffle. 'All right – here are the shoes – but
they'll be the last I'll mend for old Mrs Shifty
if she doesn't pay up!'

Ma Shuffle took the shoes and disappeared into the scullery. Shuffle heard her
muttering something, and he grinned. 'Up
to her tricks, I suppose. Good old Ma!'

After a while Ma Shuffle came out with the
shoes. The tongues looked very highly polished, though the other parts of the shoes were
muddy and dull. Shuffle scratched his head.

'Ma! What have you done to the tongues?'

'That's *my* business,' said his mother. 'Now
you mend those shoes.'

Shuffle mended them. Mrs Shifty came to
them, and Shuffle spoke sharply to her.

'One pound, please.'

'Dear, dear, now – to think I've left my
purse at home!' said Mrs Shifty. 'I'll be in
tomorrow, Shuffle. Are you there, Ma? I
hope you're coming to our meeting this
afternoon!'

'I'll be there,' said Ma Shuffle. 'I like to hear tongues a-wagging. Yes, I do!'

She went to the meeting. Mrs Well-I-Never was there, and Mrs Tuck-In, and Dame Dandy. Mrs Shifty was there, of course, because she simply loved to hear herself talk. She had changed her shoes, and put on her mended ones. She nodded to Ma Shuffle when she came in.

The meeting began. It turned out to be a most peculiar one. Every time Mrs Shifty began to speak somebody spoke and inter-rupted her – and yet nobody knew who it was.

'I think,' began Mrs Shifty, 'I really think –'

'She *can't* think,' said a voice suddenly. 'The woman's got no brains.'

'No heart either,' said another voice. There was a dead silence. Everybody looked at everybody else. Who had spoken?

'Somebody is being very rude,' said Mrs Shifty, feeling angry.

'Fancy *her* talking about rudeness!' said a voice again. 'Did you hear her being rude to old Mrs Doodle this morning?'

'Well, I never!' said Mrs Well-I-Never, astonished. 'What's happening?'

'It's somebody under the table,' said Mrs Tuck-In. But there wasn't anybody there.

'Let's get on,' said Mrs Shuffle who didn't seem quite as astonished as the others. 'We have here a bill to discuss from the builder, and another from –'

'Well, don't give it to Mrs Shifty then,' said the strange voice. 'She'll say she left her purse at home –'

'Or else that she hasn't got any change –'

'Or maybe she'll say she'll settle it next week –'

'But *she'll never pay at all*,' squealed the voices together, and went off into shrieks of laughter.

Mrs Shifty turned very pale. She got up. 'I'm going,' she said. 'I won't stay and hear these horrible things.' And she went out of the door.

'Here we go,' said a voice, as she went down the path. 'Left the meeting in a huff now!'

'All because she didn't like hearing the truth!' said the other voice. Mrs Shifty stopped in panic. Why, the voices were still with her! And they stayed with her all the way, making loud remarks all the time.

She had to pass little Shuffle's cottage on the way. He was at his front gate.

'Good afternoon,' he said.

'Good afternoon,' said the voices in chorus. 'Has she come to pay your bill?'

Mrs Shifty rushed by, scarlet in the face. 'Going at a good pace now, aren't we?' said one voice.

'Yes, fine,' said the other. 'Whoops! We nearly stepped on one of Ma Shuffle's cats. I say – I'm coming undone.'

'Well, down we'll go then,' said the first voice. And down they went, when Mrs Shifty trod on her loose shoelace and sat down in a hurry. She sat there, crying, frightened and full of astonishment.

'Here's little Shuffle running to help her up,' said the second voice. 'Good little fellow he is. I'd be ashamed not to pay my bills for his good work, if I were Mrs Shifty.'

'Shuffle – take me into your cottage. I must get away from these voices!' cried poor Mrs Shifty. Shuffle took her into his kitchen. He gave her a cup of tea.

'What's the matter?' he said. Mrs Shifty looked all round to make sure nobody could hear her.

'I think I must be going mad,' she whispered. 'I keep hearing strange voices. Don't tell anyone. Sh! Even walls have ears!'

'And shoes have tongues!' squealed the two voices together, and cackled with laughter. 'Yes, shoes have tongues!'

Mrs Shifty looked down at her shoes. The tongues shook a little, but didn't say anything.

'So *that's* it!' she said. 'Shoes have tongues

– and someone has set them wagging! It's Ma Shuffle, I know it is. Oh, I'm ashamed. I'm upset. I want to run away and hide.'

'Well, don't,' said Shuffle cheerfully. 'Pay your bills, be honest and straight and kind, and you'll have nothing to be ashamed of, Mrs Shifty.'

Mrs Shifty opened her purse and paid all she owed little Shuffle. 'Look at that,' said one of the voices mournfully. 'She's paid up. We shan't be able to talk about her if she does things like that.'

Mrs Shifty said nothing. She went home and took out all her shoes. She meant to be better from that very hour – but she wasn't going to leave anything to chance.

She took the tongues out of all her shoes, yes, every one of them, and put them in the dustbin.

'Talk to the potato parings and the cabbage leaves!' she said. 'As for me – *I'll* go and talk to old Ma Shuffle.'

Chapter 7

Ma Shuffle Comes Home

'I don't like leaving you to look after yourself for a week, it's a fact I don't,' said Ma Shuffle to little Shuffle. 'But your aunt's ill and I must go to her.'

'Ma! Anyone would think I was six years old, the way you talk,' said Shuffle. 'I'm just as able to look after myself as you are. You go along, now. I'll manage fine.'

'See you have your meals properly, and don't you forget to let the cats out at night, and remember to wind the clock – and ho, bless us all, I've forgotten to wash out my magic apron!' cried Ma Shuffle.

'I'll do that for you,' said Shuffle. It was a curious apron, one his mother wore whenever she wanted her work done quickly. It made her sing loudly, move quickly, and get her work done in half the time.

'Well, here it is,' said Ma Shuffle, and she threw it over a chair. 'See you hang it on the line to dry when there's a good wind. Now, goodbye – and don't forget to put down the cats' milk, and –'

'Shoo, Ma, shoo! You'll miss the bus!' cried Shuffle, and pushed her out of the door.

Well, for a week Shuffle looked after himself. He looked after the cats, too. They got so fond of him that they all tried to go to sleep on his knee at once, and he was for ever pushing them off.

'I'll be glad when Ma comes back this afternoon,' he told them on the Saturday. 'She's got a lap big enough for three cats. I haven't.'

He cleaned the kitchen. He cut some bread and butter. He bought a cake. He put the kettle on to boil. Aha! Ma would see that he could look after himself all right.

Ma Shuffle came bustling in, glad to be home again. She beamed at little Shuffle, and beamed at the singing kettle and the purring cats.

'Nice to be back again,' she said. 'I'll make us a cup of tea.' They had tea together, and then Ma got up. She went to the peg behind the door to get her apron – but it wasn't there.

'Where's my apron?' she said. 'You said you'd wash it for me, Shuffle.'

'Well, and so I did,' said Shuffle. 'Let's see now – I brought the washing in from the garden – but I can't remember what I did with it.'

'It's still in the washing-basket, then,' said Ma Shuffle, and she went to open it. But when she pushed back the lid she cried out in surprise:

'What's this – potatoes!'

'Oh my!' said little Shuffle. 'Yes, I remember now – I couldn't find the potato box when I got home with the potatoes, so I popped them into your washing-basket, Ma. I've been looking for them all the week.'

'What's in the potato box, then?' said Ma Shuffle. 'There it is, under the sink.' She went over to it.

'You've put all the knives and forks here,' she said. 'The *knives and forks* – you know they're kept in the table drawer, Shuffle.'

'Yes, I know,' said Shuffle. 'But it was so full I couldn't get them in, Ma.'

Ma Shuffle went to the table. She pulled out the drawer. A terrible smell came out, and Tib, Tab and Tubby, the three cats, leapt up on the table at once, mewing loudly.

'Fish! FISH!' cried Ma Shuffle, and pushed the cats off the table. She stared at Shuffle, who went bright red.

'I *wondered* where I'd put that fish,' said poor Shuffle. 'I hunted for it everywhere. You see, the larder shelf was full, Ma, and I couldn't leave it out on the table, because of the cats – and I remember now, I just pushed it into the drawer quickly, meaning to get it out and cook it for the cats' tea.'

'Why was the larder shelf full?' said Ma in

surprise, and she opened the larder door. On the shelf lay a dustpan, a duster and two brushes, and beside them stood the kitchen pail.

'Shuffle,' began Ma in a choking voice, 'look here. What's all this?'

'Good gracious!' said Shuffle. 'So *that's* where I put the dustpan, brush and pail. I couldn't find them anywhere today.'

'But *why* put them here?' asked Ma Shuffle.

'Let me see now – oh yes, there was something in the cupboard where they usually go,' said Shuffle, getting nervous. 'There really was, Ma. There was no room for these things.'

Ma Shuffle opened the broom cupboard door. Out fell a whole stack of boots and shoes! Shuffle gave a joyful cry.

'Oh! So *that's* where I put the boots I mended on Thursday! Hurrah – now I can deliver them.'

'And *why* didn't you put them into the big linen bag I made for you to carry round your boots and shoes?' asked Ma Shuffle. 'Why put them in the broom cupboard? And *what* have you put in the linen bag? The meat for Sunday – or my best hat? Or perhaps you even thought it was a good idea to put one or two saucepans in there?'

'Ma! Oh, MA! I remember now,' cried little Shuffle. 'Of course! I took the linen bag out into the garden to collect all the washing on the line – because, you see, the washing-basket was full of potatoes.'

'And where is the linen bag?' asked Ma, looking all round. She caught sight of a bag hanging on the scullery door. She went across to it.

'Here it is,' she said, and began to pull out the washing. But her apron wasn't there. Little Shuffle looked very nervous again.

'Oh, Ma,' he began. 'I seem to remember something else. Ma, I must have thought the bag was your rag-bag, the next day when I saw it. And I remember taking something out of it to wipe up the floor.'

'Not my apron!' wailed Ma Shuffle. 'My magic apron! You wicked boy! What did you do with it?'

'I only wiped up the floor – and yes, I cleaned the windows, too – and I may have used it for a dishcloth – and I know I tore a bit off to bind up my hand when I cut it,' said Shuffle mournfully.

Ma Shuffle pounced on a dirty-looking rag in the sink. She shook it out. 'My apron!' she cried. 'My magic apron! Shuffle, you just wait for a minute – just stand there, and wait. I'll wash you in the sink with my poor apron, I'll squeeze you dry, and I'll peg you up on the line by your big ears. You just wait!'

But he didn't wait. When Ma Shuffle looked round he wasn't there. He'd put himself somewhere very safe – and let's hope he's remembered where it is or he certainly won't be found again!

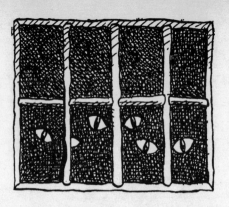

Chapter 8

The Six-Eyed Jingy-Bang

Once little Shuffle went to see his cousin Popalong. Popalong wouldn't open the door at first, and when he did he looked so scared that Shuffle was astonished.

'Oh! it's you! Come along in,' said Popalong. 'I thought you were Fee-Fi-Fo.'

'What, the goblin?' said Shuffle. 'Why should you be scared of *him*?'

'Well, he once did me a good turn, and now I just can't get rid of him,' said Popalong. 'He keeps coming in for meals, he borrows money from me, he takes my vegetables, he . . .'

Shuffle listened and his green eyes gleamed. 'Popalong, let me help you! Fee-Fi-Fo once turned Ma's three cats into logs, and we very nearly threw them in the fire before we found out what he had done, and changed them back into cats again. I wouldn't mind giving Fee-Fi-Fo a scare at all.'

'Nothing scares *him*,' said Popalong gloomily. 'He's coming tonight, worse luck – and my larder will be bare and empty when he's gone!'

'I'll come after tea,' said Shuffle. 'And if you do and say just what I tell you, you'll soon be rid of Fee-Fi-Fo!'

He ran home, chuckling. 'Ma!' he shouted, as he burst in at the door. 'Can I borrow Tib, Tab and Tubby again? And your kettles and saucepans? And have you any paper bags?'

'Bless us all! Are you crazy, Shuffle?' said his mother in astonishment. 'You can't have my big saucepan. It's got soup in it.'

Shuffle took all the others, though! First he collected all the paper bags he could find and stuffed them into his pockets. Then he tied the kettles and saucepans together with string, and hung them round his neck.

He had a hurried tea, and then set out for Popalong's house, the three cats following him with their tails in the air. Popalong heard the jingle-jangling noise and came to the door in surprise. Little Shuffle grinned. The cats waved their tails.

'We're going into your little shed,' said Shuffle. 'But before we go I'm going to tell you what to say to Fee-Fi-Fo when he hears peculiar noises tonight. Now listen . . .'

Popalong listened. He laughed. He smacked his hands together in delight. He danced round his kitchen. Aha, what a joke!

Shuffle led the three cats into the shed. It was getting very dark in there. He made the cats sit down on a bench in a row, close together. He took out his paper bags and put them ready. He settled his kettles and saucepans comfortably round him. He talked to the cats, and told them what to do. Then he waited.

At six o'clock, when it was dark, Popalong heard what *he* was waiting for – a loud bang at the door. BLAM! That was the goblin Fee-Fi-Fo, of course. Popalong opened the door. In came Fee-Fi-Fo, sniffing to smell what Popalong was going to have for supper that night.

Now in the middle of supper a frightful noise came from the little shed outside. Fee-Fi-Fo almost jumped out of his skin.

'Fee-ow! Fee-ow! Fee-Fi-Fo-eeow! FEE-Ow!'

'Who's that calling my name in such a peculiar way?' said Fee-Fi-Fo nervously. 'I don't like it.'

'Don't worry. It must be the Six-Eyed Jingy-Bang in my shed,' said Popalong. 'I've got him shut up there because I don't think he likes goblins. For all I know he eats them for his dinner. You know what Jingy-Bangs *are*, Fee-Fi-Fo – always gobbling up something or other!'

'I don't know anything about them,' said Fee-Fi-Fo in alarm. 'Never heard of one in my life. Are you sure it can't get out, Popalong?'

'It might burst the door down, of course,' said Popalong. 'What a horrible yowl that is, isn't it? Fe-ow, Fee-ow, Fee-Fi-Fo-eeow! I can't help thinking that the Jingy-Bang must guess you're here.'

The Jingy-Bang chose that moment to make another frightful noise – a jangling and clinking and clanking that made Fee-Fi-Fo leap out of his chair. It was little Shuffle dancing madly round the shed, of course, setting all his kettles and saucepans clanking and banging round him.

Fee-Fi-Fo turned pale. Popalong patted his arm. 'Don't worry. He never, never eats good kind goblins.'

That didn't comfort Fee-Fi-Fo at all. He knew perfectly well that he wasn't good or kind. The Jingy-Bang went on clanking out in the shed, and the howling of 'Fee-ow, Fee-ow' went on, too. And then the bangs began.

'Pop! BANG! Bang! POP!'

Fee-Fi-fo reached for his hat. This was too much for him! Popalong caught hold of his arm. 'No, no, Fee-Fi-Fo. Don't be scared. The Jingy-Bang always jingles and goes pop-bang. He's safe in the shed. He won't come after you.'

POP-Pop! that was two more paper bags being blown up and burst by little Shuffle out in the shed. The cats were startled too, and yowled all the more. Popalong suddenly wanted to laugh, and he could hardly bear to look at Fee-Fi-Fo's alarmed face.

Then little Shuffle went mad. He danced round the shed, clanking and banging, he popped his bags, and then he fell over a flowerpot and howled with pain. Fee-Fi-Fo gave a howl, too, and fled out of the door. As he passed the shed, the three cats leapt up to the window-sill and sat there, to watch him go. All he could see of them were their six gleaming eyes.

'Ow! It *is* a Six-Eyed Jingy-Bang!' cried poor Fee-Fi-Fo, and leapt over the wall and ran for his life.

Popalong went to the shed. He sat down on a flowerpot and cried with laughter.

'Oh my, oh my! You're the best Six-Eyed Jingy-Bang I have ever heard in my life, little Shuffle!' he said, wiping his eyes. 'Come on

in – Fee-Fi-Fo's left all his supper – and I've got some kippers for the cats.'

With their sides aching with laughter the cousins went indoors, the three cats following.

'Well, Fee-Fi-Fo's gone – and he won't come back!' said Shuffle taking off three kettles and two saucepans. 'My word – I *did* enjoy being a Six-Eyed Jingy-Bang. I'd do it all again for ten pence!'

Well, here's *my* ten pence, little Shuffle! Now you can do it again!

Chapter 9

Three Go Up a Ladder

One day little Shuffle was walking along with his friend Button when they suddenly saw somebody coming through the woods towards them.

'Look – it's Grabbit!' said Shuffle in alarm. 'Where shall we hide!'

'Why should we hide?' said Button in surprise. 'Grabbit won't hurt us.'

'He'll hurt *me*,' said little Shuffle. 'Didn't I tell you how I took him to Dame Dandy's and he fell into her Blue Spell and came out all blue? Look, you can see his nose – it's still blue!'

Grabbit's nose was certainly a peculiar sight, as blue as a forget-me-not. He stalked along, his arms behind him, an ugly fellow with a scowl on his face.

He saw Button and Shuffle, and grinned. Aha! He'd been waiting to meet that scamp Shuffle for a very long time. Now he'd pay Shuffle back for the trick that had been played on him. Grabbit hid behind a tree, and waited for the two brownies to come along.

But Shuffle was scared. He wasn't going to go anywhere near Grabbit if he could help it.

What could he and Button do? If they ran, it wouldn't be much good. Grabbit had much longer legs. If they hid, that wouldn't be much good either. Grabbit would find them sooner or later.

'Look,' whispered Button, 'there's a ladder over there, Shuffle. A woodman must have been along, pruning some trees – and he's left his ladder lying there till he comes back. Let's put it up against a tree and climb up. Grabbit won't see us then.'

So the two of them dragged the ladder to a high tree and put it against the trunk. Grabbit watched them!

His greedy little eyes shone. 'What are they doing with that ladder? Something secret, something they don't want anyone to know! They don't know I'm spying on them!'

He watched Shuffle and Button go up the ladder. Then he came out and stared at it.

'I know what they are up to! They're hiding something up that tree! Yes, and what are they hiding? All the money the two rogues have saved through mending shoes! What a find for *me*!'

He rubbed his horny hands together and walked up to the foot of the ladder. He could hear Button and Shuffle whispering together, hidden in the topmost branches.

'Ho there!' he called, in such a loud voice that the two brownies almost fell out of the tree. 'I can see you! And what's more I know what you're doing up there, too.'

'Well, tell us!' called down Button, boldly.

'You're hiding money up there,' shouted Grabbit. 'Don't deny it – I know you are! Nasty little misers!'

'We're not!' shouted Shuffle.

'Oh yes you are,' yelled Grabbit. 'And I'm coming to get it! You're going to show me where you've put it, or I'll turn you into kippers and give you to your Ma's cats to eat!'

Shuffle gave a sudden grin and nudged Button in the ribs. Button looked surprised. He was even more surprised when Shuffle began to wail loudly.

'Don't come up, Grabbit, don't, don't! Don't take our money! It isn't hidden here, I tell you. Don't come up!'

'I'm coming!' cried Grabbit, and the ladder shook as he began to climb it. 'Telling me stories like that! I'll get that money – yes, and I'll spend it, too! You won't make me go blue again, I can tell you that!'

'Don't rob us of our money!' wailed Button and Shuffle together, both with broad grins on their faces. 'Go away, Grabbit, go away!'

Grabbit soon appeared beside them, his big nose looking very blue indeed. 'Now then – where have you put the money?' he demanded. 'In a hole?'

There was a hole in a branch just above Shuffle's head. He looked at it. Grabbit saw him.

'Aha – is it in *that* hole?' he cried, and climbed up to it.

'No, no – it isn't there, don't look there!' shouted Shuffle. That made Grabbit all the more certain that there *was* something hidden there, of course. Up he went and began to scrabble about in the hole.

And down went Button and Shuffle, scrambling along the tree-trunk, sliding down the ladder to the ground. The two looked at one another and Button gave a giggle.

'Quick – take it away!' he whispered – and the two of them took the ladder from the tree and flung it on the ground!

Then they ran home as fast as ever they

could, leaping into the air whenever they thought of greedy Grabbit hunting in a hole for money that wasn't there – and trying to climb down a ladder that wasn't there either!

Grabbit was astonished to find only a few old leaves in the hole. He was even more astonished to find Button and Shuffle were gone.

'Where's the money? And where are *you*? My word, I'll be after you, you little toads!'

But the ladder was gone, and there was nobody to help him. He had to stay up in the tree, yelling and wailing, till Sniff the Goblin happened to come by – and he charged two gold pieces to drag the ladder to the tree for the angry Grabbit to climb down.

Shuffle met him the next day, and called out to him: 'Hey, Grabbit! What did you do with the money you found in the hole in the tree?'

And Grabbit went purple in the face with rage – all except his nose, which is still bright blue!

Chapter 10

Shuffle's Party

"Ma,' said little Shuffle, 'on Wednesday we shall have been here exactly a year – here in Tiptop Village. It's been a good year, hasn't it?'

'It has,' said Ma. 'We've done good business, we've made good friends, and we'll do a good deed to round off the year. We'll give a party!'

'Oooh, *Ma*!' said little Shuffle, pleased. He liked parties. 'Shall we have jellies – and will you make a cake?'

'I will – and we'll put one big red candle on it to mark the one year we've been here,' said Ma.

Well, when Tiptop Village heard that Ma Shuffle was to give a party to celebrate their first year in the village, they decided to go shares.

'*We'd* like to celebrate your coming, too,' said Dame Scary. 'Little Shuffle is a very fine cobbler, and many's the kindness you've done in our village, Ma Shuffle!'

'We'll have a party in the village hall,' said Mrs Tuck-In. 'And we'll ask everyone – yes, even Grabbit and Sniff, though goodness knows they don't deserve a treat, the miseries!'

Now, when the day came everyone was there in their very best. Balloons hung down from the walls, tossing about as people walked below. There were crackers set out on the tables. There were sixteen different kinds of sandwiches, enormous jellies that wobbled excitedly in their dishes, and dishes piled high with Mrs Well-I-Never's very nicest buns.

And right in the very middle of the biggest table was Ma Shuffle's cake, iced in pink and white, decorated with sugar violets, and with one enormous red candle in the very middle, waiting to be lit.

You should have heard the noise as everyone walked in! And then, when everyone was there, *Somebody* else came!

He hadn't bee invited. Nobody liked him. Nobody wanted him. He was the Enchanter Big-Brows from Frowning Hill, a perfect nuisance and a tiresome pest.

BUT – he knew so much magic and so many spells that everyone was very careful indeed not to offend him. He had once changed one of his servants into water, and poured him into a basin. It was very lucky indeed that the plug had been in, or that would have been the end of the servant.

And now here was Big-Brows, his wonderful silver cloak flowing round him, glowering at everyone.

'Why didn't you invite me?' he thundered.

Shuffle shivered with fright. 'Please, sir, you're so grand, and so important, we didn't like to,' he stammered. 'Aren't you supposed to be the c-c-c-cleverest enchanter in the world?'

'Of c-c-c-course I am,' said Big-Brows, mocking poor little Shuffle. 'Shall I show you some of my magic? See what happens to people who offend me!'

And to everyone's horror he pointed at Ma Shuffle, Mrs Well-I-Never and Mrs Shifty – and they changed into cowering mice! If

Tib, Tab, and Tubby, Ma Shuffle's three cats, hadn't known who the mice really were, that would certainly have been the end of them.

'Ma! Ma!' squealed Shuffle, Big-Brows laughed. He pointed at the mice again, and they turned back into the three old women.

'Don't you dare do that again,' said Ma Shuffle fiercely to Big-Brows. 'Ho, you think you're clever, don't you? Well, you're not as clever as my grandad was! He always said it was easy to change others – but hard to change yourself! Aha – you couldn't change *yourself* into a mouse!'

'Madam, I am not so foolish, with three cats about,' said Big-Brows, 'but I'll certainly do a *little* changing for you! Hey presto, wheeeeeee!'

And he suddenly changed himself into a wolf and went howling among the guests. They were just running away in fright when he changed into a horse and began to kick out at everyone. Then, hey presto, he was a green fire burning in the middle of the room.

'Wonderful!' cried Ma Shuffle. 'But any clever enchanter can do those things. My grandad could do better than that! If I stood near by and called out different things, he could change himself as fast as I could shout!'

'Call, then, call!' said the enchanter, appearing as himself for a moment. 'And when you've finished *I* shall call. What will *you* all change into then? Aha! A swarm of bees to make me honey? A flock of birds to sing to me? A copse of trees to give me wood for my fire?'

'No, no!' wailed everyone, really afraid.

'Call!' commanded Big-Brows; and Ma

Shuffle called: 'A chair! A table! A rabbit! A fox! A cushion! A clock! A pencil! A cup! A teapot!'

Big-Brows had disappeared. In his place came all the things that Ma called, one by one.

'I can find magic for everything!' cried the enchanter's mocking voice. 'Call! Call!'

Little Shuffle caught sight of the big red candle in the middle of the iced cake. His eyes suddenly gleamed. 'I'll call, Ma, I'll call!' he shouted. '*I'll* call something he can't change into!'

'Call then, call!' cried Big-Brows.

'Light the candle on the cake!' shouted Shuffle, holding up the dish with the cake on it. 'Make yourself the flame to light this candle! You can't do *that*!'

But immediately there came a flame on the candle – the enchanter could even turn himself into that!

Phoooooooo! That was little Shuffle blowing out the flame. It was gone! There was a dead silence – and then what a clamour!

'You've blown him out!' He's gone, he's gone! Flames never come back once they're blown out. He's gone, he's gone!'

So he had. Nobody ever saw Big-Brows again, and certainly nobody wanted to.

'Hurrah!' they all yelled.

They had a wonderful party – but do you know, nobody lit that candle again! They cut the cake and ate it – but they didn't light the candle.

Well, *I* wouldn't have either, if I'd been there! Would you?

Chapter 11

Round and Round it Goes

Ma Shuffle was polishing her kitchen stove and listening to little Shuffle talking to Mrs Whine-A-Bit.

'It's downright kind of you to mend my shoes for me so quickly, little Shuffle,' said Mrs Whine-A-Bit. 'And for nothing, too, because I'm so poor. Now I wonder what I can do for you in return. I've no eggs to give you. And, dear me, there's not even a lettuce in my garden I can offer you. And –'

'Ma! You tell Mrs Whine-A-Bit we don't want anything in return for a bit of kindness,' called little Shuffle.

Ma turned round and looked with her sharp eyes at Mrs Whine-A-Bit. '*We* don't want anything,' she said. 'But a bit of kindness should never be wasted, Mrs Whine-A-Bit. You know that as well as I do. If you can't return it to the one who gives it to you, well, pass it on.'

'That's right,' said Shuffle. 'It's bad luck to keep a bit of kindness. You should either return it or pass it on. Good morning to you, Mrs Whine-A-Bit.'

The customer went out with her shoes. Ma Shuffle laughed. 'Do her good to pass on a bit of kindness instead of one of her whines!' she said. 'I wonder if she'll remember.'

Well, Mrs Whine-A-Bit *did* remember. She met Mr Tuck-In, stalking along looking very grand indeed. Just as he passed her he dropped his purse. It fell open and his money rolled everywhere.

Mr Tuck-In was fat and he didn't like stooping. Mrs Whine-A-Bit was pleased to think she could pass on the bit of kindness so soon. She hurried to pick up the money, and gave it to Mr Tuck-In.

'Thank you, my good woman. Very kind of you,' he said. He felt in his purse for a piece of money to give Mrs Whine-A-Bit.

'No, thank you, Mr Tuck-In,' she said. 'It

was a very small kindness I did you. Don't pay me for it. Just pass it on!'

She went down the road, delighted with herself. Mr Tuck-In was surprised. He went home and found his wife trying to patch up an old bonnet. He told her about Mrs Whine-A-Bit, and how she had told him to pass on the little kindness.

'*Well!*' said Mrs Tuck-In, her eyes shining, 'pass it on to *me*, my love – I do so badly want a new hat!'

Mr Tuck-In was just going to say something rude about new hats when he stopped. That would be passing on a bit of *un*kindness – most unlucky. So he smiled pleasantly and nodded.

'Yes. You go and get a new hat, my dear!'

'Oh, you generous man!' cried Mrs Tuck-In, and flung her arms round him. 'What can I do for you in return?'

'Nothing, nothing, nothing,' said Mr Tuck-In, rather grandly. 'It's a very small piece of kindness, my love – just pass it on!'

Mrs Tuck-In hurried to the hat shop, looking for someone to pass on the kindness to before she forgot. She only met one person, and that was old Mr Tappit with his stick. He was standing at the kerb trembling as he always did when he wanted to cross the road.

Mrs Tuck-In hurried to him. She took his arm and guided him safely across.

'Now that's kind of you,' said cross old Tappit, surprised. 'You come along to my house and I'll give you the biggest lettuce you ever saw.'

'I haven't time,' said Mrs Tuck-In. 'So just you pass on the bit of kindness instead, Mr Tappit. Don't forget!'

Well, Mr Tappit wasn't used to doing kindnesses of any sort and he couldn't for the life of him think what to do. So he did the easiest thing he could – he went up to a small child pressing her nose against a toy shop window and gave her twenty pence.

'Go and buy a toy,' he said, and felt surprised at the nice warm feeling that came inside him.

'Oh, Mr Tappit, thank you! Shall I come and weed your garden for you – or take your dog for a walk?' said the little girl.

'No, no. I'll whisper in your ear what to do,' said Mr Tappit. 'There's a little chain of kindness going about just now – pass it on, will you, and don't break the chain!'

The little girl didn't buy a toy. She remembered Mrs Clang, the blacksmith's wife, who was ill. 'Twenty pence would buy an enormous bunch of yellow daffodils!' said the little girl to herself, and she skipped over to the flower shop.

Mrs Clang could have cried for joy when she saw the yellow daffodils.

'Why, they make me feel better already!' she said. 'The flowers, and your bit of kindness! You come along when I'm better and I'll make you a chocolate cake.'

'No, Mrs Clang,' said the child. 'This bit of kindness has got to be passed on. So you pass it on to someone else, then we shan't break the chain.'

Mrs Clang worried about that when the little girl had gone. How could anyone in bed pass on a bit of kindness? At last she called her husband and showed him the daffodils.

'Look there,' she said. 'Little Mary-Lou brought these, the kind little thing. And it's a bit of kindness I want to pass on. But how can I do that while I'm lying ill in bed? You pass it on for me instead, will you?'

'Right,' said big Mr Clang, and he sat down and thought hard. What could he do?

He suddenly smacked his hand down on the bed.

'Ah, that's it, of course! I'll pop over to Ma Shuffle's. The chain of her well is broken, and she and little Shuffle can't get it mended. They have to go to the end of the lane for water each day, the poor things. I can mend it for them in a jiffy.'

And so, to Ma Shuffle's great surprise, there was Mr Clang out in her backyard mending the chain of her well bucket. What a wonderful thing!

'No charge, Ma, no charge at all!' called big Mr Clang. 'Just passing on a bit of kindness that seems to be floating around!'

Ma Shuffle looked at little Shuffle. Her eyes shone. 'Do you know, I wouldn't be surprised if that's your bit of kindness come back to you,' she said.

'Well,' said little Shuffle at once, 'we'll keep it going, Ma – we'll PASS IT ON!'

80

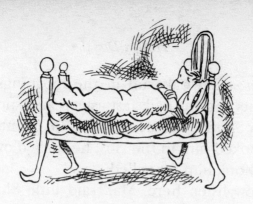

Chapter 12

Snoozy Comes to Stay

When little Snoozy's mother asked Ma Shuffle if she'd have him to stay for a week or two whilst she went away, Ma Shuffle wasn't very pleased.

'He's a lazy fellow, that boy of yours,' she said to Mrs Snoozy. 'A real lie-abed, I call him. I've got no use for people like that.'

'Oh, he'll be all right with *you*,' said Mrs Snoozy. 'He's promised me he'll be up and about when little Shuffle is. He'll help you a lot, Ma.'

'He'd better!' said Ma. 'My son's busy at his cobbling in the mornings, so I shall want your Snoozy to go and do the shopping for me.'

Well, Snoozy didn't. He was the laziest, sleepiest-looking brownie you ever saw. He just *wouldn't* wake up in the mornings! He lay there in his bed, fast asleep and snoring. If Ma Shuffle shouted at him, he grunted. If she poked him in the ribs, he turned over. If she shook him, he yelled.

'Now listen here, Ma,' said little Shuffle. 'Don't you go off and do your shopping tomorrow as you did today, and leave that lazy creature in bed. You rub a spell on the bed's feet. Go on!'

Ma Shuffle gave a sudden grin. She went to her cupboard of spells and took out a tiny box of blue ointment – and before she went to bed that night she rubbed some on each foot of Snoozy's bed!

In the morning she called Snoozy. 'Hey, get up, Snoozy! Your breakfast is ready. I want you to go shopping for me. There's the fish to get, and the bread to fetch, and the old chair to come back that's been mended, and the cabbage from the greengrocer, and . . .'

But she might just as well have been talking to the chest of drawers, for all the notice Snoozy took. Little Shuffle looked at his mother and grinned. They both stood peeping in at Snoozy's bedroom.

The bed creaked. It groaned. It put out a foot and tapped the floor with it. It put out another and scraped the floor. It did a little dance on all four, but Snoozy didn't stir.

'Right. You can go,' said Ma Shuffle, and the bed began to walk towards the door. It was a small, narrow bed and it squirmed out easily. It creaked loudly.

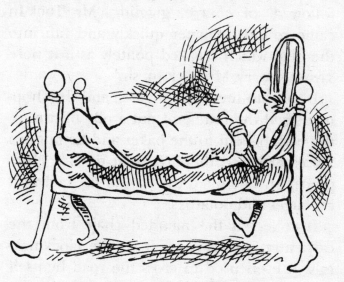

'It's laughing!' said little Shuffle and he laughed, too. 'Ma, where's your shopping list?'

'Here,' said Ma, and she put it on the pillow. 'Get along now, bed.'

The bed squeezed out of the front door.

Snoozy was still fast asleep, his head buried in the pillow. The bed managed the steps quite nicely, and even stepped over one of the three cats, who was sunning herself there. Then it set off down the street.

It met quite a few people. They were full of amazement to see the bed stepping along with somebody fast asleep in it. The children followed, of course, giggling. Mr Tuck-In came round a corner quickly and ran into the bed, which creaked politely as if it were saying, 'Sorry, Mr Tuck-In, sir.'

It went to the fishmonger's, and the shopman read the note and put a pile of fish on the bed. It went to the baker and he put two loaves of bread there. It went to the greengrocer and he piled the foot of the bed with cabbages and potatoes.

It collected the mended chair from the carpenter, and a clock from the clockmaker's. It even tried to cross the road by itself and nearly got run over. A car hooted loudly, and the bed almost tripped over as it dashed back to the pavement in a hurry.

The noise and the jolt woke up Snoozy. He flung back his arms, stretched and yawned. Then he sat up.

Good gracious! He must be dreaming! He *couldn't possibly* be sitting up in his nightshirt in a bed that was trotting along a street in the middle of Tiptop Village. And what was this on the bed – cabbages – and potatoes – and bread – and, POOH! What could that be? Fish!

People ran beside the bed, giggling. Children called out: 'Get out of bed and play, Snoozy. Come and play!'

But Snoozy couldn't possibly get out of

bed in his nightshirt, he was much too ashamed. He lay down and covered his head up with a sheet. The children pulled it off. Somebody tucked the packet of fish beside him in bed.

POOH! That was too much. Snoozy gave a yell, leapt out of bed and ran for home, his night-shirt flapping against his legs, and the bed trotting after him, creaking as if it were out of breath.

He flung himself into little Shuffle's kitchen, crying with shame. Ma Shuffle looked up in surprise.

'Why, Snoozy! Where have you been? Surely you didn't go out shopping in your night-shirt!'

The bed squeezed in at the door and creaked politely.

'Look at that now,' said little Shuffle. 'They've brought the shopping back between them. Well, well – do you often go shopping in bed, Snoozy?'

Snoozy went sobbing into his bedroom, followed by the bed. He shook his fist at it. 'Hateful thing! Miserable thing! If you ever do that again I'll chop you up for firewood and old iron!'

'Creeee-ee-eeak,' said the bed, and leaned against the wall as if it were tired.

Well, that was the last time that Snoozy was ever sleepy again in the morning. At the very first creak of the bed he was up and dressed! Dear me, even if it was the wardrobe creaking, he was out of bed like a shot.

His mother was very pleased to find Snoozy so changed when she got back from her visit. 'What's happened, Snoozy?' she said, but he wouldn't tell her.

His name isn't Snoozy now. It's Jiffy. You can probably guess why – it's because he gets up in a jiffy!

Chapter 13

Sniff Gets into Hot Water

'I don't want to do the washing!' said Sniff the Goblin.

'You're a lazy, good-for-nothing little goblin!' scolded his mother. 'It will do you good to bend over the washtub and rub and scrub, and then hang up the wet clothes on the line! Now I'm off to catch the bus. Fill up the tub, Sniff, and get the soap!'

His mother went off to the bus. Sniff grumbled and groaned and went to get the hot water to fill the tub.

Somebody popped his head round the door. 'Hello, Sniff! Hard at work again? I say – you're not going to do the *washing*, are you?'

'Mind your own business, Pippy,' said Sniff in a huff.

'Do you know what *you* want?' said Pippy. 'You want a washing-spell! Ma Shuffle's got a beauty. She's put it into a big scrubbing brush, and my, you should see it work!'

'What does it do?' asked Sniff.

'Well, it rubs and scrubs all the dirty clothes all by itself, rinses them under the tap, and even hangs them on the line,' said Pippy. 'I saw it when Ma Shuffle lent it to my aunt once. It's a wonder.'

Pippy began to whisper. 'Sniff! Don't say I told you – but little Shuffle's taking it to Dame Scary this morning, to help her with her spring cleaning. Why don't you – er – just *borrow* it for a bit?'

Sniff stared at Pippy in delight. 'Yes! I will! Ma Shuffle scolded me once, and I'll pay her back by borrowing her magic brush. Hooo! That'll be fine!'

He ran out to the gate and watched for little Shuffle to come by. Ah, here he was, whistling as usual, carrying a bag of mended boots and shoes – and with his Ma's big scrubbing brush under one arm!

Sniff hopped out of his gate, leapt on the surprised Shuffle and grabbed the brush. He was indoors in a trice, and banged the door behind him.

'Hey!' called Shuffle in a rage. 'That's my mother's brush. It's magic. Bring it back!'

The door was locked. Shuffle looked in at the window, very angry indeed.

Sniff put the brush into the hot water and swished the soap round and round till a big lather came. 'Do your work, brush, do your work!' he cried, and piled in a heap of dirty clothes.

My word! You should have seen that magic brush! It grew a dozen bony little hands all round itself. It seized the clothes, and soaped and scrubbed them. It washed them up and down, and Sniff had to jump out of the way because the brush made big splashes on the floor.

'Good brush, then, fine brush,' said Sniff, as if he was talking to a dog. He was delighted. The brush suddenly leapt out of the tub, dragging the soapy clothes with it, and off they went to the tap.

In a trice they were being rinsed clean.

The brush wanted to take the clothes to the line outside, and hang them up to dry. But it couldn't because the door was shut

and so were the windows. So it flung the things down on the table, and pattered about on its funny little hands.

Then it pulled up the rugs and put them into the tub! It tore down the curtains, and in they went, too! It even put Mrs Sniff's red cushion into the soapy water and began to scrub and wash and squeeze for all it was worth.

Sniff was most alarmed. 'Here, you brush!

That's enough! You did the washing – now stop!'

The brush didn't take a scrap of notice. It dragged everything to the tap and rinsed them and squeezed them.

Little Shuffle was still looking in at the window. He was dancing about in delight, laughing like a woodpecker. 'Ha ha ha, ho ho ho! Go to it, brush, go to it!'

The brush saw Mrs Sniff's best hat on a peg behind the door. To Sniff's horror, that went into the dirty water, too.

After that the brush just went mad. It kept trying to take everything out of the door to hang on the line and, as it couldn't, it went rushing round looking for more things to wash.

Into the tub went the kitchen stool, two kettles and the clock. In went the apple pie Mrs Sniff had baked for dinner. Sniff howled in rage, and ran to the brush. He tried to grab it – but instead the brush grabbed *him*!

He went into the dirty black water, too, and the brush began to scrub him and squeeze him, and rub soap all over him. Sniff yelled and struggled – and little Shuffle held on to the window sill and laughed till he cried. Oh, what a joke! Oh, if only Ma was there to see all this!

The brush dragged Sniff to the tap and he screamed as the cold water poured all over him. 'Help, little Shuffle, help. It'll drown me!'

Shuffle ran round the house and found a window a little open. In he went. He rushed into the kitchen, and stopped in dismay

when he saw the flood of water there. 'I'll have to open the door and let it all out!' he cried.

So he unlocked the kitchen door and out went the water. And out went the brush, too, with Sniff the goblin, and pegged him firmly on the line by his great big ears! There he swung in the wind, howling.

The brush hurried back and dragged out all the things it had washed – my, how peculiar they looked swinging on the line – especially Mrs Sniff's best hat!

Shuffle called to the brush:

'Brush, you've worked with might and main,
Be still again, be still again.
Riminy-rominy-ripple-a-dee,
Brush, come over here to me!'

And hey presto, there was the brush back again under little Shuffle's arm. He stood and grinned at poor Sniff shaking in the wind, pegged up by his goblin ears.

'Tell me when you want to borrow Ma's brush again,' he said. 'And just remember, Sniff – when you set magic things to work, be sure you know the words to stop them when they've finished! Good-day! Give my best wishes to Mrs Sniff.'

And off he went, whistling, the brush tucked under his arm. 'Sniff will be on the line till his ma comes home!' he chuckled. 'And then, dear me – he'll certainly find himself in hot water again.'

Chapter 14

Ma Puts on her Thinking-Cap

Rat-tat! Rat-tat!

'Who's that knocking at everyone's door?' said Ma Shuffle, looking out of the window. 'My, my – it's Mr Plod the policeman!'

So it was. He looked very solemn and serious, too, as he stood at each door, saying something in his deep, slow voice.

He came to Ma Shuffle's door. Rat-tat! She opened the door.

'Well, you're doing a lot of hammering this morning, Mr Plod,' said Ma. 'What's it all about?'

'It's about the stealing and the thieving that's going on in Tiptop Village,' said Mr Plod. 'Eggs taken, crops taken, tools taken out

of sheds. Very serious business, Ma Shuffle. It's my job to catch the thief. I'm asking everyone if they have any idea who it is.'

'Oh yes – I've quite a good idea!' said Ma. 'But I've got no *proof*, Mr Plod – and you won't catch me accusing anyone till I've got real proof!'

'Quite right, Ma, quite right,' said Mr Plod. 'Well, now – can you help me to find the thief, do you think – without naming any names or pointing any fingers? You're clever, Ma. How can we find the thief?'

'Come back tonight and I'll tell you,' said Ma. 'I'll put my thinking-cap on, and maybe I'll know how to catch the thief!'

As usual, her thinking-cap worked very well indeed!

When Mr Plod came to see her that night Ma told him how she would catch the thief.

'Now, you listen to me,' she said. 'Little Shuffle is going to put my cat Tubby into our garden shed. You're to get every single person in Tiptop Village here, Mr Plod, and they are to go into the shed one by one, and stroke my cat.'

'But whatever for?' said Mr Plod, amazed.

'You're to tell them that Tubby will yowl out loud when the thief strokes him,' said Ma. 'Oh, he'll yowl like ten cats rolled into one! And we'll all hear him, for we'll be standing outside the shed – *and we'll know who's inside, Mr Plod!*'

'Extraordinary!' said Mr Plod, staring at Ma in amazement. 'Yes, yes, Ma Shuffle. I'll certainly bring everyone here.'

'Little Shuffle looked at Ma when Mr Plod

had gone. 'Oh, Ma! Honestly, Tubby won't know.'

'Be quiet – and fetch Tubby here,' said Ma. 'You can watch what I do to him – and maybe you'll guess how he'll tell me the thief.'

Six o'clock the next evening came. Tubby was put into the shed on a box and told to sit there quietly. 'You're going to have a lot of fussing, Tubby,' said Ma. 'You'll enjoy that!'

Mr Plod came, followed by a long line of silent and astonished villagers. There were Mr and Mrs Tuck-In, Dame Scary, Mrs Whine-A-Bit, Mrs Well-I-Never, Sniff the Goblin, Button the Brownie and his mother, Grabbit, Mr Clang the blacksmith and his wife, Popalong, and many others.

Ma nodded to Mr Plod. He turned and spoke to everyone very solemnly. 'Now, we are here tonight, as you know, to find the thief of Tiptop Village.

'Tubby, Ma's cat, will tell us who he is. Each of you is to go alone into the shed and stroke Tubby from head to tail once, twice, or as many times as you like. He will make no noise except to purr – until the thief strokes him!'

'Aha! Then he'll *yowl*,' said Ma. 'He'll yowl and we'll all know who the thief is. Come along now. In you go, one by one.'

In they went, Mr Tuck-In first. He stroked Tubby vigorously. *He* wasn't afraid of making him yowl! Mr Tuck-In was an honest man.

Mrs Tuck-In went into the shed, and then Mrs Well-I-Never. No yowling was heard, but just a soft and contented purring. Tubby was enjoying all this stroking!

Grabbit went in and stroked Tubby gently. He knew he wasn't the thief, but he was a bad fellow and he was a bit afraid of making Tubby yowl anyhow. But no, Tubby didn't. He just purred.

Well, will you believe it, every single person went into Ma's shed and came out again, except, of course, Ma herself and Mr Plod – and yet Tubby didn't yowl. No, he didn't give even the very smallest yowl!

'There! I told you Tubby wasn't clever enough,' said little Shuffle. Ma nodded to Mr Plod again.

'Stand in one long row, please,' said Mr Plod. 'There is still one more thing to be done.'

So everyone stood in a row and Ma and Mr Plod went down the line – and they said a most peculiar thing!

'Show me your hands, please, palms up!'

And everyone showed their hands – and, will you believe it, they were as black as soot! Yes, what a surprise, as black as soot!

But it wasn't really astonishing because, you see, Ma had rubbed Tubby with black soot from head to tail – so that everyone who stroked him had black hands afterwards!

But no – not everyone had – who was this with white hands? Who was this holding out trembling hands as clean and white as could be?

'Sniff the Goblin!' cried Ma, and she held up his hands for everyone to see. '*You're* the thief! I guessed you were – you mean, snivelling little creature! You're the thief!'

'How do you know?' wailed Sniff in terror. 'Tubby didn't yowl, he didn't, he didn't!'

'No, because you were too afraid to stroke him!' said Ma. 'You knew *you* were the thief – and you were afraid Tubby would yowl as soon as you touched him! So you didn't stroke him, as everyone else did – and your hands stayed clean and didn't get sooty.'

'Come with me,' said Mr Plod to Sniff, and howling dismally, the nasty little goblin went off with the big policeman.

'And everyone else can come with *me*!' said Ma briskly. 'I've got hot water and soap and towels for you all! We'll soon get rid of the soot. Tubby, you come too!'

Little Shuffle washed Tubby clean, and whispered in his ear: 'You found the thief all right, Tubby – but do tell me, *would* you have been clever enough to yowl if Sniff had stroked you?'

'E-owee-ow,' said Tubby obligingly. So now you know the answer.

Chapter 15

All Upside Down

Button the Brownie came running into little Shuffle's kitchen.

'Shuffle! What am I to do? Grabbit's moved into our cottage, and he won't get out! His horrid sister, Mrs Well-I-Never, is with him.'

Little Shuffle stared at Button in dismay. 'Button! What will your mother say when she comes home from her holiday? She'll have nowhere to go – and all her nice things will be spoilt.'

'I know,' wailed Button. 'And I daren't go there either – so I can't do any work. I shall *starve.*'

'No you won't. You can come and stay with me,' said Shuffle. 'It's a pity my ma's away –

she might give us a spell to get Grabbit out of your house.'

'Ooooh,' said Button, cheering up. 'Yes – a spell. Where does she keep them? Can you get one?'

'No. She keeps them locked up,' said Shuffle. 'Anyway I wouldn't take one without asking her.'

'Oh. Well, what are we to do then?' asked Button, looking dismal again. 'Think, Shuffle, think. You have such very clever thoughts sometimes.'

Shuffle sat down and thought. Button watched him anxiously. He saw him scratch his head. He saw him scratch his nose. He saw his eyes begin to twinkle, and his mouth begin to smile.

And then little Shuffle leapt up, slapped his hands on his knees, took hold of Button and danced him round the kitchen till he almost fell over.

'You've had one of your clever thoughts. I know you have,' panted Button. And little Shuffle certainly had.

He told Button his plan, and Button laughed till he cried. Then the two of them got a large sheet of paper and printed some big words on it:

BEWARE!
The Upside-down people
are here!
Beware! They can't be
seen and they can't be
heard, but they are here
BEWARE!

'That looks good,' said Shuffle. 'I hope we've spelt all the words right. Now let's go and put it up near your cottage.'

So out they went when it was dark and put up the big notice. They looked through the lighted windows of Button's cottage and scowled to see Grabbit and his unpleasant sister there.

In the morning, Shuffle and Button went

out and heard everyone talking excitedly about the mysterious notice. 'It was near my house,' said Grabbit. 'What do the Upside-Down People do? I've never heard of them.'

'Well, if they're the ones I'm thinking of, they walk all over your ceilings and walls,' said Shuffle solemnly, 'and they hang down from them, quite invisible, and wait for people to pass by. Then they grab.'

Grabbit was fond of grabbing things himself, but he wasn't at all pleased to hear of somebody else who might grab *him*. He went off looking scared.

That day Button and Shuffle were very busy. Do you know what they did?

They got together all the boots and shoes and slippers that Shuffle had there to mend, and they rubbed them in the soot that came down Ma Shuffle's chimney when they put the brush up the flue! Well, well, well!

And then they popped all the boots and shoes into two big baskets and carried them in the dark up the hill to Button's cottage, where Grabbit and his sister still were. Then they hid under a bush and waited.

Presently the gnome and his sister came out. 'We'll just walk down to the village to get a few things,' said Grabbit, and off the two went.

'Now – quick!' said little Shuffle, and he and Button went to the front door. Button unlocked it with his key and in they went.

'The ladder – hurry!' said Shuffle.

'Here it is!' said Button, and brought the step-ladder into the kitchen.

'You do the ceiling, I'll do the walls,' said Shuffle with a giggle. 'Use all the shoes there are – in pairs, of course!'

Shuffle took a pair of slippers, coated underneath with black soot. He pressed them first on the floor from the door to the wall, and they left black footprints!

It looked as if someone had walked over to the wall. Then Shuffle pressed them all the way up the wall!

Button giggled and nearly fell off the ladder. 'It looks as if somebody has gone across the floor and walked straight up the wall, Shuffle,' he said. 'Now look – I'm doing footprints on the ceiling, too – all the way across!'

He had a pair of sooty boots on his hands and he walked those boots across the ceiling. Shuffle squealed with laughter. He took another pair of shoes and walked them across the floor again and up another wall.

By the time those two had finished, the floor, walls and ceilings were covered with black footprints. It looked very strange to see them going up the walls and across the ceiling!

'Ooooh! The Upside-Down People have been here all right!' said Button, with another giggle. 'I'll put the ladder away. We'd

better go. Shuffle, it looks too strange for words. When I look up at those footprints I feel quite giddy!'

They hid outside under a bush. Grabbit and his sister came back, and went indoors. They lit the lamp again – and then Mrs Well-I-Never gave such a scream that Grabbit jumped.

'Grabbit! Look, look!'

Grabbit looked. He saw the footmarks going up the walls – and across the ceiling – dozens and dozens of them! He clutched his sister and looked all round fearfully.

'It's the Upside-Down People!' he hissed. 'They may be hanging upside down from the ceiling now. Quick – we must go before they grab us! QUICK!'

Without even waiting to get their bags the two shot out of the cottage, ran into a bush in the darkness and fell over Shuffle and Button.

'*Got you!*' said Shuffle in a horrible sort of voice, and Mrs Well-I-Never screamed.

'They're here! The Upside-Down People are here – they grabbed my legs!' she squealed. She and Grabbit fled down the hill at top speed.

Shuffle and Button rolled over and over on the grass, laughing. 'You're wonderful, Shuffle,' said Button at last. 'I wish I had clever thoughts like you.'

'Well, I've just had another,' said Shuffle, getting up. 'Let's go and wash off those sooty footmarks before your mother comes home. *She* wouldn't think them clever at all!'

But *I* think they were, don't you?

Chapter 16

Dame Dandy's Umbrella

'Now, I'm just off,' said Ma Shuffle, tying her bonnet-strings. 'I'll only be gone two days, so you can't get into much of a muddle in that time, little Shuffle.'

'No Ma,' said Shuffle, busy hammering a nail into a boot. 'Have a good time!'

'And Shuffle – you *will* remember to take back that umbrella of Dame Dandy's, won't you?' said Ma. 'The one she lent me this morning. I promised she should have it today.'

'I'll remember, Ma,' said Shuffle. 'You'll miss your bus if you don't go right away.'

'Well, *don't* forget about the umbrella,' said Ma. 'You never know what anything belonging to Dame Dandy will do, if it's left lying about. Goodbye, Shuffle.'

Off she went. Little Shuffle got on with his work, and the three cats sat and watched him. He whistled softly. He liked working – it was nice making old things new again.

He forgot all about the umbrella till the next day. He wouldn't have remembered it then if it hadn't spoken to him. It had a dog's head for a handle, and it spoke quite suddenly, in a barking voice.

'Woof! Lazy boy! Why didn't you take me back?'

Shuffle jumped. So did the cats.

'WOOF!' said the umbrella again, and its little dog-mouth opened and shut at the top of the umbrella handle.

'Goodness! It's *you* talking!' said Shuffle, in astonishment. 'I forgot all about you. You're a nuisance! Now I shall have to take you back all the way to Dame Dandy's.'

'Lazy creature!' said the umbrella, and gave him a sharp poke. It stared round at the three cats, who were sitting down watching it. It suddenly growled loudly and opened itself out with a click.

The cats streaked out of the door in a hurry. 'Now stop it,' said little Shuffle. 'I don't allow umbrellas to behave like that.'

He caught hold of it and shut it. He tapped the dog's-head handle. 'No more rudeness from *you*!' he said, and walked off to Dame Dandy's with it.

But when he got there, the door was shut and there was a note pinned to it: 'BACK TOMORROW.'

'Bother!' said Shuffle. 'Well, I'll have to stand you here in the porch, umbrella. Dame Dandy will see you when she comes home.'

'I don't want to be left here,' called the umbrella in alarm. 'Take me with you.'

But Shuffle had run off down the hill. He sat down at his work when he got in, and soon the mended boots and shoes began to pile up in heaps.

There came a knock at the door. 'Come in!' cried Shuffle. But nobody came. Shuffle got up and opened it.

In hopped the umbrella, whining a little. 'You shouldn't have left me. It's a long walk back!'

'What! You've come here to me again!' cried Shuffle in a rage. 'I won't stand it!' He chased the umbrella round the kitchen, but it kept tripping him up. At last it stood itself in a corner, quite quietly.

'Well, you just stay there, then,' said little Shuffle angrily. 'And don't let me hear a sound from you all day!'

That umbrella was a perfect nuisance. It hopped at the cats, barking, and opened itself out every time Tib, Tab or Tubby came into the kitchen. They didn't even dare to drink their milk.

'All right,' said Shuffle, and he picked up the umbrella suddenly by the handle. 'Out you go – into the rubbish heap where umbrellas like you belong.'

And he stuck it firmly into the middle of the rubbish heap, with just the dog's head showing.

But soon there was a tap-tap-tap at the door again – and in came that umbrella, smelling of all the rubbish in the heap!

'I think you're unkind to me,' it said mournfully. 'I feel ill. Let me stay with you.'

'Certainly *not*,' said Shuffle in disgust. 'Out you go.'

He threw the umbrella out into the yard. It was now pouring with rain, and the umbrella opened itself at once. It hopped round on its dog's-head handle, getting wetter and wetter and wetter.

Then it peeped in at the window. It saw little Shuffle sitting in his mother's armchair, fast asleep by the fire, with a newspaper open in his hands. The three cats were on his knee.

The window was open just a crack. The umbrella shut itself, hopped up to the sill and squeezed itself through the crack.

'I'm cold. I'm wet,' it whined, and hopped over to little Shuffle. 'Move over, you cats. Let me come up there too!'

The cats yowled and leapt off Shuffle's knee at once. He woke up in a hurry and found himself very wet indeed. The dripping umbrella was on his knee.

'This is too much,' said Shuffle angrily. 'Into the dustbin you go!'

And into the dustbin it went, and the lid was banged down on top of it. No more was heard of the umbrella for a long time.

In fact, little Shuffle forgot all about it, and he hopped into his warm bed, cuddled his hot-water bottle and went to sleep with Tib, Tab and Tubby on his feet.

What was that noise on the window? 'Tap-tap-tappitty-tap! Let me in. I'll break the window if you don't!'

It was that dreadful umbrella again! It had jiggled off the dustbin lid. It had hopped out, and come to the window. It was covered with potato peel and tea-leaves, and it was very cold and very cross.

Shuffle grumbled and groaned, and the cats hissed and spat. It wasn't a bit of good. 'Tap-tap-tappitty-tap, let me in, I'll break the window, tap-tap-TAPPITTY-TAP!'

Shuffle opened the window. 'You wretched, tiresome thing! Go and stand in the corner,' he said, and got back into his warm bed.

But the umbrella crept in beside him, cold and wet and smelly. It dug its dog's head handle into him. 'Cuddle me,' it whined. 'I'm cold.'

But little Shuffle wouldn't. Cuddle a knobbly, spiky, smelly, wet umbrella – no thank you! He got out of bed, pulled the eider-down over him and went to sleep on the floor. Tib, Tab and Tubby curled up with him, so he was warm, but most uncomfortable.

And that tiresome umbrella slept peacefully in poor Shuffle's bed all night long. He's going to take it back to Dame Dandy today. I hope she's home again now, don't you?

Chapter 17

Spreading the News

'Good-day, Ma Shuffle!' said Dame Scary, and she popped her head in at the door.

'Come along in, do,' said Ma. 'That's right. Now, sit down and have a cup of tea with me. Put your bag on the window sill or it will get all mixed up with little Shuffle's cobbling. Two lumps of sugar or three?'

'Oh, only *one*,' said Dame Scary, who was such a timid little person that she never dared to take more than one lump even when she was alone at home.

They sat and talked till the kitchen clock struck twelve. Dame Scary leapt up at once. 'Oh, my! I must go. I've my old aunt coming to see me.'

Off she went out of the door. Ma Shuffle yelled to her. 'Hey, Sally Scary! You've left your bag on the window sill!'

Dame Scary was just passing the window when she heard Ma's shout. She put her head in at the window and reached for her bag. She smiled and nodded at kind Ma Shuffle, and went home to get ready for her old aunt.

Little Shuffle was out spending the day with Button the Brownie. He came home at two o'clock bursting with news.

'Ma! Mr Plod the policeman's gone along to Dame Scary's house. What's happened, do you suppose?'

'Good gracious! Poor Sally Scary – she'll be shivering like a jelly to see Mr Plod walking up to her front door!' said Ma Shuffle.

'And I met Mr Snooper, and he said he wasn't a bit surprised to hear the news,' said little Shuffle. 'And Mrs Whine-A-Bit said it served Dame Scary right, and Mrs Tuck-In said –'

'What in the world is this all about?' demanded Ma Shuffle, and she put her bonnet on at once.

She and Shuffle went off together to

Dame Scary's little cottage. What a hulla-baloo there was when she got there!

Mr Plod was leading poor Dame Scary down her front path, and quite a crowd of people were watching. Dame Scary was sobbing and crying.

Ma was most astonished. 'What's it all about?' she asked.

'Ma,' said Mr Plod solemnly, 'have you missed your bag – with all your money in it, and your keys and your stamps?'

Ma looked at Mr Plod as if he was quite mad. She shook her head.

'Ma,' said Mr Plod, even more solemnly, 'you bag's gone – and I can tell you where it is!'

'The man's crazy!' said Ma Shuffle. She turned to little Shuffle. 'Run home and get my bag,' she said. 'You know where I keep it. Telling me fairy stories about my bag – you ought to be ashamed of yourself, Mr Plod!'

Little Shuffle raced off like the wind. He was soon back with a very large bag. Everyone gaped. They knew Ma Shuffle's bag all right.

'I t-t-t-t-told him I hadn't t-t-t-t-taken it!' wept Dame Scary.

'Now Sally, cheer up and tell me all about it,' said Ma, putting her arm round Dame Scary, and pushing the surprised Mr Plod away.

'I'll tell you, Ma,' said Mr Plod, suddenly looking round at everyone very fiercely. '*I'll* tell you. And, when I've told you, SOME-BODY'S going to get into trouble over this.'

'Well, go on and tell me,' said Ma.

'See Mrs Busy-Body over there?' said Mr Plod, pointing. 'Well, she came to the police station and reported that Dame Scary had been seen taking your bag from your window sill!'

'Well,' said Mrs Busy-Body, the feather in her hat wagging busily as she spoke, 'well, I thought such a thing *should* be reported. Mrs Tuck-In told me – and she's too kind to report such a thing to the police – so I thought, well, *somebody* ought to –'

'So you hurried off in glee,' said Ma. '*I* know, you Mrs Busy-Body.' She turned to Mrs Tuck-In, who was looking very upset.

'How *can* you say such a wicked thing about Dame Scary?' she said.

'Well – Mrs Well-I-Never told *me*,' said Mrs Tuck-In nervously. 'She did, as true as I stand here. Didn't you, Mrs Well-I-Never?'

Mrs Well-I-Never tried not to be seen, but Ma's sharp eyes soon found her. 'Come out here, Mrs Well-I-Never!' she called. 'Why are you hiding? Are you ashamed of something?'

'How was I to know it was an untruth?' said Mrs Well-I-Never. 'Didn't I meet Mrs Whine-A-Bit in the grocer's, and didn't she tell me all about it? How Dame Scary came along by your cottage, peeped in at your window, saw your bag on the window-sill, and stole it away!'

'Did she say all that now!' said Ma Shuffle. 'Mrs Whine-A-Bit, you're clever to see a thing that didn't happen!'

Mrs Whine-A-Bit pushed Mr Snooper forward rather roughly. 'It's not *my* fault!' she whined. 'Mr Snooper came up to me and told me every word. He *did*, Ma – said he'd seen Dame Scary steal your bag and go off with it.'

'And I suppose he said she tucked it under her shawl, and looked all round to make sure no one had seen her, and then ran off at top speed?' said Ma scornfully.

Mrs Whine-A-Bit looked surprised. 'Yes, he did! Didn't you, Mr Snooper?'

Mr Snooper was afraid of Ma. He shuffled his feet and went red. 'I *did* see Dame Scary put her hand in at your window and take out a bag,' he said.

'Yes – and that's all you *did* see, you great big exaggerator!' said Ma. 'Sally Scary had just had a cup of tea with me, and rushed off without her bag. I shouted to her, and she popped her head in at my window, and picked up her own bag. HER OWN BAG, I said.'

Nobody said a word. Mr Plod coughed. 'Er – this is very serious,' he said. 'To blacken somebody's character – and er –'

'Mr Plod, I think you had better go and arrest Mr Snooper,' said Ma. 'Nasty old poke-his-nose-in-every-where!'

But Mr Snooper had vanished. 'Well,' said Ma, 'what about going for Mrs Whine-A-Bit? Bless us all, she's gone, too! Well, there's Mrs Well-I-Never, Mr Plod – she could do with a bit of a shock from you.'

'She's gone as well, Ma,' said little Shuffle. 'Look, she's at the end of the lane.'

'Get Mrs Tuck-In, then,' said Ma, and she looked round. 'Why, she's disappeared, too – and whatever's happened to Mrs Busy-Body?'

They were all gone, ashamed and very much afraid of Mr Plod and Ma. The two winked at one another solemnly.

'You tell Mr Snooper I want a word with him,' said Ma to Mr Plod, tucking her bag under her arm, and patting Dame Scary on the back. 'I'll come and see him tomorrow.'

But Mr Snooper wasn't in when she

knocked at his door. He'd packed his bag and gone.

I don't blame him. I'd do the same if Ma Shuffle was after *me*!

Chapter 18

Well, it Served them Right

'Are you going to take those boots and shoes out this morning?' Ma called to little Shuffle. 'Well, then, will you deliver these three wishing spells to Dame Dandy for me?'

'Right, Ma,' said Shuffle. He put the mended boots and shoes into a basket and set off, whistling. The wishing spells were in a little yellow packet on the top of the boots. Shuffle kept looking down at it to make sure it was still there.

'Can't lose wishing spells,' thought little Shuffle. 'Very dangerous if they got into the hands of the wrong people.'

Now, as he went through the wood, along came Grabbit the Gnome, and with him was his sister, Mrs Well-I-Never. They both stopped at once.

'Well, I never! There's little Shuffle large as life and twice as natural,' said Mrs Well-I-Never.

'Being a good boy and taking back all his mended boots and shoes,' said Grabbit. 'And how are all your mother's cats, Shuffle?'

Shuffle didn't like this. He began to edge away. They came closer – and Mrs Well-I-Never's sharp eyes caught sight of the little yellow packet on top of the basket.

'Well, I never! If that isn't one of Ma Shuffle's packets of spells. Let me see, Shuffle.'

And before little Shuffle could stop her she had snatched the yellow packet and opened it. Out came the three tiny wishing-spells.

Mrs Well-I-Never knew what they were at once. 'Grabbit!' she said, giving them to her brother. 'Look here – *wishing* spells. We've never had any in our lives.'

'Give them back,' said Shuffle, feeling very uncomfortable indeed. 'They won't do you any good. Ma says however much people like you are given good things like wishing spells, you'll only get bad out of them. So you give

them back before anything horrid happens
to you.'

'Are you being rude to us, Shuffle,' said
Grabbit. 'Sister, he's being rude. Shall we
wish him away to the Land of Dustbins?'

Shuffle was scared. 'Er – is it worthwhile
wasting a wish on me, do you think?' he said.

'On the whole, no,' said Grabbit. 'Come on
now, sister – what are we going to wish for? A
grand castle set up on that hill over there?
My, that would make our friends stare!'

'A grand castle!' snorted Mrs Well-I-Never. 'Just like a man, Grabbit. Who's going to do the work in a great, cold, draughty castle? I'm not going to live there and scrub your floors and cook your dinners, and –'

Mrs Well-I-Never could quite well go on like this for hours. Grabbit yelled at her.

'All right, all right. We won't have a castle. *You* think of something.'

'I wouldn't mind a few new hats,' said Mrs Well-I-Never. 'I saw one yesterday with –'

Grabbit did such a loud snort that all the rabbits who were watching darted back to their holes.

'Hats! HATS! Just like a woman. What do you want a hat for with a head like yours, and a face like, like –'

'Mr Tappit's goat,' said little Shuffle, before he could stop himself.

'*Oh*!' said Mrs Well-I-Never, in a rage. 'Well-I-Never! Well-I-never-did-in-all-my-life! Grabbit, we must use a wish on Shuffle. We must, we must. What shall we wish? Shall we wish him into an earwig and tread on him? Shall we wish him into a worm and call that fat thrush down? Shall we wish him into a nail in our shoes and walk on him all day long? Shall we –?'

'Hold your tongue,' said Grabbit impatiently. 'You're full of crazy nonsense. Always have been. I do wish, for once in your life, that you'd be sensible.'

Shuffle gave a squeal of laughter. All the watching rabbits pricked up their ears.

'*Now* what's so funny?' demanded Grabbit.

'You've wished a wish,' grinned Shuffle. 'You wished she'd be sensible for once.'

Mrs Well-I-Never gave a scream. 'Yes, you did! You did! Look at the wishing spells in your hand. One's gone!'

Grabbit looked – yes, there were only two wishing spells left now. Mrs Well-I-Never grabbed at them and got them.

'There now – you can't waste any more. I've got them both. You be careful, Grabbit. I've got two wishes here – you just be careful.'

Grabbit lost his temper. He ran at his sister and she screamed and ran between the trees. 'Don't shake me! Don't! Oh, Grabbit, I wish you'd go away.'

Shuffle gave another squeal of laughter. Mrs Well-I-Never looked at him. '*Now* what's the matter with you?'

'He's gone. You wished him away,' said Shuffle. 'I say, this is as good as a play. Do go on.'

'Where's he gone?' she said.

'If I knew I wouldn't tell you,' said little Shuffle. 'Good riddance, I say.'

'But – but – he's my *brother*,' said Mrs Well-I-Never. 'He's not a good brother – but he's the only one I've got. I want him back. Where can I go to look for him?'

'You might try in the Land of Crazy People – or maybe you'd find him in the Land of Grab and Snatch, wherever that is,' said Shuffle, enjoying himself. 'Or possibly in the Land of Rubbish. Or –'

'Don't' said Mrs Well-I-Never, in tears. 'I didn't mean to wish him away. We shall never see him again. Poor, poor Grabbit.'

'Well, *I* can put up with that all right,' said Shuffle cheerfully. Then he felt sorry for Mrs Well-I-Never.

'Look,' he said, 'have you forgotten the wish that Grabbit wished?'

'Of course I haven't,' said Mrs Well-I-Never. 'A really silly wish – he wished I'd be sensible for once.'

'Well, *be* sensible,' said Shuffle. 'Use your

last wish and wish Grabbit back if you want him so badly. But personally I should think a few new hats would be a much better wish for you.'

'Well, I never! To think I didn't think of that!' said Mrs Well-I-Never, cheering up. 'Of course – I've still got a wish left. Grabbit, I wish you back!'

And back he came, frowning and furious. He had been in the Land of Rubbish and it wasn't nice.

Shuffle disappeared, grinning. Well, well, let them argue it out between them. He'd better go back and get three more wishing spells to take to Dame Dandy.

'Ma's right. She said if you gave good things to bad people they would only make bad come out of them,' he said. 'Scoot off, you listening rabbits – the show's over.'

Chapter 19

Mr Dozey's Dream

Mr Dozey lived just outside Tiptop Village in a dirty little tumble-down cottage. He was a fat and lazy fellow who never did a day's work if he could help it.

One day he had a very pleasant surprise. Mr and Mrs Tuck-In were giving a party – and they asked everyone in the village – even old Dozey! The postman put his invitation through his letter box, and he was *most* surprised when he opened it.

'A party! I haven't been to one for years,' said Dozey. 'The thing is – what am I to wear? I want a new coat and waistcoat and a new pair of trousers and a hat and pair of shoes. Can I borrow them from anyone?'

But nobody would lend old Dozey

anything. They had got tired of that years ago. Whatever they lent Dozey never came back!

Everyone said the same thing to him when he came asking for clothes for the party. 'Dozey – you go and do what everyone else does – you work a bit, and earn some money to buy your own clothes!'

Dozey was annoyed. 'How mean they are!' he said to Blinks, his cat. 'Not a scrap of kindness in them. Well – I've a good mind to go along to old Ma Shuffle and borrow a spell. If she'd give me a Change-a-Bit Spell I could use it on my old clothes, and change them into new ones.'

This seemed a very good idea indeed to Dozey. He appeared at Ma's door, and smiled and bowed.

'What do you want?' said Ma briskly. 'Come to ask for a job of work? Well, you go into my garden and do a bit of weeding – and you might sweep the path while you're about it – and there's a corner over there that wants digging – and –'

Dozey was horrified. What – do all that work! What was Ma thinking of?

'I came to borrow a Change-a-Bit Spell,'

he said. 'I want to change these old clothes of mine into nice ones for the party.'

'The only reason I'd lend you a Change-a-Bit Spell is to change you from a lazy, sly old fellow into a hard-working, decent one,' said Ma sharply. 'If you want new clothes, earn them. Get along now! I'm expecting a visitor – my brother, Mr Rumbustious. He'll soon send you packing if you're round here when he comes.'

Dozey didn't like Mr Rumbustious, so he walked off, annoyed. He went through the woods, muttering to himself.

It was a very hot day, and Dozey soon felt tired. He sat down under a bush and went to sleep. He dreamed a wonderful dream. In his dream he had a marvellous new suit of clothes, from a hat with a feather in, to a blue silk vest and shoes to match.

And will you believe it, when he awoke, the very first thing he saw hanging on a tree near by was a fine suit of clothes, with a feathered hat, a vest, trousers, shoes and coat! Dozey was too astonished for words.

'My word! Look at that! My dream's come true. I'm a lucky fellow today, no doubt about that! Ha! I'll dress myself in these and

then go and show myself to old Ma Shuffle!'

So he took off his own things and threw them down. He dressed himself in the smart new suit of clothes and felt very grand indeed.

He strode to the nearby pond and looked at himself in the clear water. 'Sir Magnificent Dozey!' he said, and bowed to his own reflection. Then he thought he would go and parade up and down the village street and let everyone see him and admire him.

Off he went, the feather waving in his hat. It was a pity he hadn't washed himself in the pool, and it was a pity too that he hadn't combed his hair that morning!

Everyone stopped and stared at this well-dressed Dozey, as he paraded up and down, nodding and bowing.

'Where did you get those clothes, Dozey?' asked little Button in surprise.

'I dreamed them and they came true!' said Dozey grandly.

'A very useful sort of dream,' said Button disbelievingly, and ran off.

After he had shown himself off for half an hour. Dozey went to Ma Shuffle's. Ho – wouldn't she stare! He wondered if her brother Mr Rumbustious was there yet. He didn't like him at all – too noisy and very rude at times to people like Dozey. Well, Dozey was certain that Mr Rumbustious had never in his life been clever enough to dream a dream that immediately came true!

Dozey thought he would peep in at the window of Ma's cottage to see if Rumbustious had arrived yet. So he went round into the garden, and was just about to peep through the window when he heard Mr

Rumbustious's enormous voice booming away inside.

'I tell you, Ma, if I get hold of that fellow I'll throw him up to the moon! The thief! The robber! The mean, sneaking fellow!'

'Well, Rumbustious,' began Ma's voice, but her brother interrupted again immediately.

'I was walking through the woods, and I was hot. I came to the pool – it looked so clear and cool. So I pulled my clothes off – my best ones, mind – and into the pool I went. And I tell you, Ma, when I came out my clothes had gone – yes, even my new feathered hat – and these filthy rags were left instead. Gr-r-r-r-r! If I get hold of that fellow, I'll throw him up to –'

'Yes. You said that before, Rumbustious,' said Ma. 'But let's think – who in the world could it have been? Who would *dare* to do a thing like that? He would have to walk away in your grand clothes and everyone would see him!'

Outside the window Dozey's knees began to knock together. His face went pale. He felt very peculiar indeed.

His dream hadn't come true! Mr Rumbustious had come along while he had been dozing, hadn't seen him and had undressed and gone for a swim – and while he was in the water, he, Dozey, had woken up and got into Mr Rumbustious's clothes. Whatever was he to do now?

'I tell you, if I catch that fellow, I'll throw . . .' began Rumbustious again, in his enormous voice. That was too much for poor Dozey. He ran to the gate – and little Shuffle saw him from the door!

'Ma! There's the thief – Mr Dozey! He's got all uncle's clothes on!' cried Shuffle, and out he went with Mr Rumbustious to catch Dozey.

Well, Dozey's knees were still knocking together, so he couldn't run very fast, and very soon he was being marched into Ma's kitchen by Shuffle and his uncle.

'I can explain it all, I can, I can,' began Dozey.

'You can explain it to Mr Plod the policeman,' said Rumbustious. 'And after that I'm going to throw you up to –'

'No, no, no!' cried Dozey in fright. He turned to Ma Shuffle. 'Ma, save me! It was all a mistake! What can I do to show you it was?'

'Oh, well, now you're talking sense,' said

Ma. 'Didn't I tell you this very morning there was some weeding to do, and the path to be swept, and a corner that wants digging – and . . .'

And that's how it came about that Mr Dozey spent three whole days working hard in Ma Shuffle's garden, with little Shuffle keeping an eye on him through the window. He's not going to the party, though – no, he doesn't like meeting anyone just now. They all say the same thing.

'Hi, Dozey! Any more dreams come true?'

Chapter 20

My Goodness – What a Joke!

One day Mrs Well-I-Never came rushing to speak to her brother, Grabbit the Gnome.

'Grabbit!' she said. 'Where are you? I've got news for you! Look what I've found.'

'What?' asked Grabbit disagreeably. 'You always find such silly things – stones with holes in, or four-leaved clovers that aren't lucky, or things that belong to someone else!'

'Well, you just see what I've got!' said Mrs Well-I-Never, and she opened her hand and showed something to Grabbit. It was a tiny box of blue powder.

'It's a Blue Spell!' said Mrs Well-I-Never. 'Dame Dandy must have dropped it on her way up the hill this morning. It's the same kind of spell that she put in her cauldron, and you fell into it and came out blue – don't you remember?'

'I'm hardly likely to forget whilst my nose is still blue,' said Grabbit gloomily. 'Throw the spell away, sister – I don't like Blue Spells.'

'No, but listen,' said Mrs Well-I-Never. 'You know we've always wanted to pay little Shuffle back for making you fall into Dame Dandy's Blue Spell – well, now we've got a wonderful way to get even with him.'

'How?' said surly Grabbit.

'Do listen, Grabbit,' said Mrs Well-I-Never. 'I'll make a cake – and I'll put this Blue Spell into it – and I'll send it along to Ma Shuffle because it's her birthday! She'll eat it and so will Shuffle – and they'll both turn blue!'

'Ha ha, ho ho!' roared Grabbit suddenly. 'That's a good joke. Oh, that's the best joke I ever heard. Make your cake, quickly!'

So Mrs Well-I-Never made the cake. It was a beauty, crammed with fruit. She shook the blue powder into it and baked it. 'It's a pity I can't ice it,' she said. 'I haven't any icing sugar.'

'Oh, never mind about that,' said Grabbit. 'Is it ready? Well, take it down to Ma Shuffle at once. Ho, ho – what will she and little Shuffle look like tomorrow? – oh, what a joke this is, what a joke!'

'Well, I never! I've not seen you so pleased for years!' said his sister. 'Well, I'll go now. And don't you give our secret away to *any*one!'

Ma Shuffle was surprised and pleased with Mrs Well-I-Never's present of a cake. 'Thank you,' she said. 'Do come to my party this afternoon and share the cake, will you?'

'Oh, no, thank you,' said Mrs Well-I-Never at once. That would never do! 'Well, happy birthday, Ma!'

'Look at that,' said Ma to little Shuffle. 'There's kindness even in Mrs Well-I-Never. What a pity she sent me a cake though – I've such an enormous one already, and it's iced so beautifully.'

'Ma, send Mrs Well-I-Never's cake to Mrs Nearby,' said Shuffle. 'We've got enough cake, really, and it's nice to be generous if we can. Mrs Nearby can't come to your party, she's not well. She'd love a cake for herself!'

'Bless your kind heart, little Shuffle,' said Ma, 'You take it along then, with my best wishes.'

So the Blue Spell cake was taken over to Mrs Nearby's by little Shuffle. Mrs Nearby was in bed and couldn't come to the door, so Shuffle pushed the cake in through the window.

'Thank you, little Shuffle, you're kind,' said Mrs Nearby. 'I'm expecting the doctor soon, and maybe he'll tell me I can get up.'

The doctor did come, very soon after that.

He was Doctor Healem, and he was just like his name. He shook his head over Mrs Nearby.

'No, you can't get up yet,' he said. 'And what's this rich fruit cake I see here on the window sill? You mustn't eat anything like that yet, Mrs Nearby.'

'Oh dear – well, will you take it away and give it to someone?' said Mrs Nearby. 'I might nibble a bit if you don't, it looks so good.'

'Yes – I'll take it to Mrs Shifty,' said Doctor Healem, and he took it away with him. But Mrs Shifty was out, so he left the cake just by the front door. She found it there when she came home.

'Look at that! Somebody has left a cake here for me!' she said. 'Well, I'd keep it, only I'm going away tomorrow and it would get stale in my larder. I'd better give it away.'

So what did she do but take it that very afternoon to Mrs Button. Mrs Button was pleased.

'Well, that's nice of you,' she said. 'I'll let little Button have it for his tea. I don't like fruit cake myself, so he can eat it all. He'll start off with five or six slices, I expect!'

But little Button was very naughty that afternoon. 'Now you just shan't have that beautiful cake!' scolded Mrs Button. 'I'm ashamed of you, spoiling your nice new coat like that! Don't you know wet paint when you see it? Don't you –'

'All right, Ma, all right,' said Button. 'I won't have the cake. Don't go on and on at me though! What shall I do with the cake?'

'You take it to Mrs Popalong,' said Ma Button. 'Go along now – and don't you go near that wet paint on the way!'

Button went to Mrs Popalong's. She was very busy baking. 'Mrs Popalong – I've brought you something from Ma!' called Button.

'Put it down on the hall table,' called back Mrs Popalong. 'I'm busy this morning, little Button. You put it there and I'll see to it when I've finished.'

So Button left the cake on the hall table – and when Mrs Popalong came along to see what he had left, she laughed aloud.

'Well, I *would* get a present of a cake just when it's my baking day and I've made six!' she said. 'It's a nice enough cake, too – but it looks a bit battered somehow, round the top.

I'll ice it when I ice mine and send it off to someone else. I know Pa Popalong won't eat any cakes but mine, so it's no good keeping *this* one!'

Well, she iced it beautifully in pink and white and put pink roses on top. Now, who should she send it to? Everyone was going to Ma Shuffle's party this afternoon – but wait! Didn't she hear Ma say that Mrs Well-I-Never and Grabbit weren't going? Well, she'd send *them* the cake then! They'd be glad of it, if they were missing the party.

So kind Mrs Popalong walked to Mrs Well-I-Never's house with the iced cake. Mrs Well-I-Never was thrilled to see it.

'Well, I never!' she said. 'I never did see such a fine cake. Did you ice it yourself, Mrs Popalong?'

'Yes,' said Mrs Popalong. 'But I didn't make the cake. I don't know who made it – little Button brought it along this morning. Well – I hope you enjoy it, Mrs Well-I-Never!'

'Grabbit!' called Mrs Well-I-Never that teatime. 'Come and have tea. Mrs Popalong's sent a fine iced cake for us!'

'Oh, good!' said Grabbit, and he sat down at the table. 'My, it certainly is a fine-looking cake. I say, sister – do you suppose little Shuffle and his Ma are sitting down gobbling up that Blue Spell cake?'

'Yes!' said Mrs Well-I-Never. 'Oh, what a joke! I'm glad *I'm* not having a bit!'

'I'm glad too,' said Grabbit, taking his second slice of cake. 'It's the best joke I ever heard in my life. Ha ha, ho ho ho! What a joke!'

Well, it was, of course – but not quite in the way they meant. By the end of tea-time they were both as blue as cornflowers!

My goodness – what a joke!

Chapter 21

Hurrah for Shuffle the Shoemaker!

'Do you know who's taken the cottage at the corner of the green?' said little Button, popping his head round Shuffle's kitchen door.

'No – who?' asked Shuffle, pricking up his pointed ears.

'Mr Pah!' said Button. 'And all I can say is – I'm very glad I don't live in Tiptop Village! I couldn't bear to have Mr Pah poking his nose into my affairs, and saying 'Pah!' to this and 'Pah!' to that.'

Ma Shuffle looked dismayed. 'Of all the people we could do without in this village, Mr Pah is the one!' she said. 'I've met him before. He'll look in here and see what little Shuffle's doing – and he'll say "Pah! What an old-fashioned way to mend shoes!" And he'll look into my cupboard of spells and say "Pah! Is that the best you have? – what a poor lot!" He just takes the heart out of you, that magician.'

'Oooh – is he a magician?' said little Button.

'Yes – and a rich one, too,' said Ma. 'He's often offered a sack of gold pieces to anyone who knows better than he does – but nobody's ever won it yet!'

'Oooh,' said Button again, and he looked at little Shuffle. 'A sack of gold, Shuffle! I wish *we* had that!'

'Well, you'll never get it, Button, so forget it,' said Ma. 'Now here's the parcel for your mother. Get along with it, and keep out of Mr Pah's way if you can!'

Mr Pah was certainly a tiresome fellow. He looked in at Dame Scary when she was washing, and said, 'Pah! If that's the way you wash, I shan't ask you to do *my* things for me!'

He poked his nose in at Mr Clang the blacksmith's, too. 'Pah!' he said.'What stupid little bellows you use to blow up your fire – no wonder it takes you ages to get it red-hot.'

'Pah!' he said to Ma Shuffle. 'What a col-
lection of old-fashioned spells you have!
Haven't you ever heard of the new ones?'

'I'd like to know a spell that would stop
people poking their noses in where they're
not wanted,' said Ma, in a dangerous kind of
voice.

'Pah! That's easy,' said the magician. 'You
just take a pinch of pepper, a sprinkle of –'
And then he caught the glint in Ma's eye,
and thought better of it. He backed out of

the door. 'I might tell you another day,' he said.

'Yes, you do,' said Ma. 'I could use a spell like that straightaway!'

Well Mr Pah was so annoying that he really upset everyone in the village. 'Can't we get rid of him?' they said to one another.

'He's so clever,' said Dame Scary dolefully. 'There's no getting the better of him.'

Button and Shuffle put their heads together. 'Listen, Button,' said little Shuffle. 'I've thought of a trick or two – not magic, you understand, because I wouldn't know better magic than Mr Pah. But just a trick or two.'

'I'll help,' said Button eagerly.

'Well, all you've got to do is to spread the news about that the wonderful enchanter, Mr Tricky, is visiting Tiptop Village, and giving a show,' said Shuffle. 'Tuesday afternoon at half-past three. Tell everyone to be there. Mr Pah will hear about it, too, and he'll be along.'

'But Shuffle – what's the trick you know?' asked Button anxiously. 'You'll have to be careful. If the trick doesn't come off, you'll get into trouble!'

'Yes, I know. But I'll have to risk that,' said

Shuffle. 'They're silly tricks I've thought of, really – but that's just why I think they'll take Mr Pah in. Now you go off and spread the news about Mr Tricky, Button!'

Well, everyone soon heard that the wonderful enchanter Mr Tricky, was coming next Tuesday, and, of course, Mr Pah heard it, too.

'Ha! A chance to show him up!' thought Mr Pah. 'A chance to show how much cleverer I am than this Mr Tricky, whoever he is!'

Everyone was on the village green at half-past three. Shuffle was there, too, dressed in a flowing cloak and a pointed hat. He had rubbed a Whisker Spell on his face, so he had a very fine beard, and didn't look at all like little Shuffle!

Mr Pah came, too, pahing and poohing as usual. He pushed his way to the front.

'I'm Mr Pah, the famous magician,' he said. 'I've never heard of *you*! There's nothing you can do that I can't. What are you going to do? What's that blackboard for?'

'I was going to teach a few spells,' said little Shuffle, and he wrote down a few simple ones on the board. Mr Pah laughed till he cried.

'Sort of thing I learnt in my pram!' he said. 'You'll be teaching us that two and two make four next.'

'Well, I wasn't going to teach that – I was going to show that six and four can make eleven, not ten,' said Shuffle, his beard waving in the wind. 'Can *you* do that, Mr Pah?'

There was a silence, as everyone listened for Mr Pah's answer.

'Impossible, and you know it,' said Mr Pah. 'No matter how you try, six and four will only make ten, not eleven. You're a silly fellow, Mr Tricky. I'll give you a sack of gold if you can make six and four into eleven!'

'Then watch me!' cried little Shuffle, and everyone craned to see what he was putting on the blackboard.

'Now look – what's this?' asked Shuffle, and he wrote down VI.

'Six!' cried everyone.

'And what's this?' asked Shuffle, and wrote down IV. 'Four!' yelled everybody.

'Now watch me make six and four into eleven!' shouted Shuffle. 'Here's my VI again – six as anyone can see – but I'm going to write my IV upside down this time – like this – ΛI – and I'll write it touching the VI –

there you are – it's now XI – and isn't that eleven?'

'Yes, it is, it is!' shouted everyone in delight. Mr Pah stared in disgust.

'A trick, that's all,' he said.

'I never said it wasn't' said Shuffle. 'That sack of gold is mine, Mr Pah! And now another challenge – can you write a word that exactly describes you – and which reads the same upside down?'

'Impossible,' said Mr Pah grumpily. 'Never heard of one in my life!'

'Well, *I* learnt it at school!' said little Shuffle, and on the blackboard in very large letters he wrote this word:

chump

'Chump!' gasped everyone. And they laughed and laughed. Mr Pah turned scarlet. He glared at little Shuffle, who was now solemnly turning the board the other way up. And lo and behold the word was exactly the same upside down. You try it!

Mr Pah stalked off, caught the next bus and never came back again. But he was honest enough to leave two sacks of gold pieces behind!

'You're rich, little Shuffle!' said everyone. 'You're a prince! You can build a castle, and call yourself Prince Shuffle.'

'I'm sharing out the gold with everyone in the village,' said little Shuffle. 'I'm no prince. I'm a village cobbler, and I'm happy in my job. Come along and help me count out the money – and this time six and four will make ten, and not eleven. No tricks *this* time!'

So he shared out all the money – and I'm really not surprised to know that when people meet him, they call out: 'Hello, Prince Shuffle!' Are you?